Part One

Fury

Prologue

It was gone ten thirty when we finished the delicious meal of fresh seafood at The Sou'Wester restaurant down in the village. We thanked Sandy, made noisy farewells and started on the walk back to the lighthouse... our lighthouse now. There was a frost already forming on the windscreens of the few cars parked in the main street and the sky was clear; millions of stars twinkling brightly like fairy dust thrown into the air. We walked briskly, our full stomachs complaining but keen to get back into the warmth of the lighthouse. I kept a close eye out for the terrifying creature I had seen earlier and that had haunted my short time in Canada, but it seemed to have disappeared; I began to relax.

As soon as we got in, mum, dad and Sal went up to bed. Dad wanted an early night after his first day in the new job and Sal said she was bored. I sat on the sofa and tried to read for a while. I could hear footsteps upstairs and sounds of people using the bathroom. The book felt heavy in my hands and I just couldn't get into the story. I felt like skimming some stones across the sea, after all, it was right on my doorstep. Hurriedly, I got back into my warm coat and scarf and started out into the freezing night air. There was a slight breeze outside and the frost was becoming thicker. I clambered over the rocks on the seaward side of the peninsula and found myself on a sloping boulder that ran into the water, the waves gently lapping at the white granite. I scouted around and soon found three or four flattish stones, ideal for skimming. Planting my feet wide, I heaved the first out into the Atlantic Ocean. It dipped quickly and sank without a trace. Disappointed, I took hold of a second stone and as I drew my arm back, there was a sound behind me. Glancing round, my eyes widened in horror as there above me, on the rocks and not more than ten metres away was the creature; a wolf; for a wolf it must surely have been, crouched on its haunches, teeth barred and ears laid back. Without thinking, I took a step back and the frost that had, without me realising, formed on the white stone took my feet from beneath me. I fell backwards and was instantly engulfed by the icy sea. My head went under and I spluttered for breath. The salt-water burned my nose and I coughed, arms flailing, trying to regain my feet. For a brief second my feet brushed against the boulder but then slipped away. Terror enveloped me as the water soaked my thick parka and its weight began to drag me down. Horrified, I realised I was about to be pulled down and drowned. I gasped a last breath before the ice-cold water closed over my head.

There was a tugging at my wrist. Something had grabbed the sleeve of my waterlogged parka and was pulling me. My feet kicked hard as I sought to push myself upwards, towards the person who was trying to save my life. Roughly, in jerking pulls, my shivering body was yanked from the sea; inch by inch, my arm stretched out above my head and my back against the rock I was dragged to safety. At last I lay gasping and spluttering, shaking uncontrollably in the icy coldness of the Canadian night.

At last, I looked up to see who my saviour was. My gaze took in the sight of the huge wolf, standing there; his head looming over me. The great beast suddenly threw back its head and began to howl; long haunting bellows that rent the night. I fought to get to my feet but my limbs wouldn't respond. The cold had drained the life from them and I knew with a sickening certainty that although I had survived the clutches of the sea, it would only be minutes before the cold finished the job. My body was rapidly losing the last of the heat it contained. The wolf continued to howl until suddenly, there was a light, flashing from side to side above and behind me and then a voice calling, 'Harry! Harry! Where are you son?'

I worked my lips, but the uncontrollable chattering of my teeth made it impossible to utter a single word. At the sound of the voice in the distance, the wolf's head, which still loomed over me, tilted down for a moment and dark eyes regarded me solemnly; and then it was gone; it vanished as if it had never been there.

'Thank God! Thank God!' the voice continued. I felt arms grab me and I was hauled up and over a shoulder. 'I've got you son. You'll be alright now.' And I knew I would.

Chapter 1
Bad News

I suppose I should explain how I came to be in a lighthouse in Canada, half drowned and terrified of the huge wolf that had attacked me; otherwise, nothing else that happened to me will make much sense. So, here goes:

How would you feel if your parents had just sat you down and told you that the whole family were moving to another country? That you were never going to see your friends again or play football for the local team? I suspect you'd be pretty angry. That's just how I felt, because it happened to me on Monday 3rd November at 4.45 p.m. I was so mad that I stormed upstairs and sat on the floor in my room with my back against the door so dad couldn't get in. How could they do that to me? I didn't want to go to Canada. I was perfectly happy right there in Windsor. In fact, I loved it there. I liked our house, I liked the castle, I liked my school, I liked our car and I liked my friends. Why would I want to go and live in Canada? I wouldn't, and I was not going. I told dad so... well... I shouted it at him actually, but I was upset.

Dad knocked on my door an hour later and I let him in even though he was the last person on Earth I wanted to talk to. He sat on the bed next to me and explained how things were. Apparently, he had lost his job the month before. He was a marine engineer. That meant he designed boats; luxury yachts actually, that cost an astronomical amount. Only super rich people could afford them. Well... what with the state of the banks, the economy and the cost of things in general, apparently those people who used to be ordering these floating palaces couldn't afford them anymore. So the company lay off over half the people who worked there; that was over eighty people, all of them with families to support.

I couldn't believe I hadn't realised something was wrong. He'd been the same old dad I'd always known; laughing, joking and playing the clown. Not that night though; when he sat next to me on my bed I could see he had been crying and his voice was trembling as he spoke to me. He told me he had been trying to get a new job; had applied for everything in the paper and at the Job Centre, just so he could get a pay packet and allow the family to stay there in our home, but nothing doing, just rejections or no reply at all. And the previous week Mum had suggested he signed on at an agency; that's a company that finds jobs for you. Sounds great, doesn't it? A company that finds a job for you. Only it's not that simple;

there was just one job for a marine engineer and guess where it was? yep...Canada.

Dad had been desperate, I can see that now. There were no jobs for him round Windsor. We would have had to move anyway; there was no way he could have afforded to pay the mortgage on our house and Windsor was ultra expensive. I would have lost my friends no matter where we moved and God knows where we would have ended up.

Dad was interviewed only the day before, online, via Skype and they offered him the job immediately. We were leaving in a few weeks on a ship. I was probably more unhappy then than when mum and dad had first told me earlier on in the day, but at least I didn't blame dad after that; I could see it wasn't his fault... but that didn't make it hurt any less.

I left for school on the morning of 4th November, before mum or dad were even up. I just couldn't face talking to them. Sal (my sister) came out of her room as I was creeping downstairs; I could tell she had been crying because her eyes were all red. She walked downstairs behind me and followed me out of the front door. We walked to school together - we never normally did that, she was fourteen and my sister after all - and she was just sobbing. Not only was Sal going to be leaving her friends behind but she had been seeing this boy for the previous three months and that

7

would be all over as well when we moved. If I'm honest, it was going to be harder on her than on me. What a couple of sad characters we must have looked. Eventually, Sal made me sit on a bench with her in the park near school. She told me that when mum and dad had first told us about the move to Canada, she had decided to run away. She wasn't going to give up her life there, it wasn't her fault dad's job had gone up in smoke and she wasn't going to pay for his problems. I was scared when she said that; obviously I disliked her; what brother doesn't dislike a sister? She's annoying and bossy and... likes girl things. But she's alright really; she was helping me out at school with this kid who started bullying me and she was always giving me some of her pocket money when I ran out so I could buy a few sweets at the end of the week. I wouldn't have wanted her to run away and leave us. When I said that to her she actually started laughing; at the same time as she was crying. After she calmed down, she put a hand on mine and said that she hadn't slept all night, just sat up thinking things through. She said she had written a list of pros and cons on a piece of paper. On the cons side she had written the reasons to stay, all the good things about her life in Windsor; her friends, clubs, boyfriend, Christmas, music and so on; fifteen things altogether. After that, she surfed the net for a while and did some research on Canada and the place we are

8

supposed to be moving to. When she had finished this she wrote the pros list, things that would be good about moving to Canada; and do you know what? It took her half an hour to write and was twice as long as the cons list. She said she just stared at the piece of paper for hours and finally she realised that it wasn't mum and dad's fault this was happening to us; they would have done anything to keep us there, where we really wanted to be but it just wasn't possible. They loved us and were doing what they thought was best for the family. She said that though she couldn't stop crying and REALLY didn't want to lose her boyfriend, she was prepared to give it a go. At the very least it would be a great adventure.

As I listened to what Sal was saying, I found myself nodding my head. I didn't want to move away from my friends, but with computers, we could easily keep in touch on Skype and even play games with each other on the PlayStation. And of course, I was sure to meet new friends over there, and I was sure I'd heard that Canada was an amazing place. Even as these thoughts were crossing my mind I felt a sort of excitement building up inside me. I wanted to get on the internet and find out more about Canada myself.

We left the park just after that. The sun was higher in the sky and the future did not look quite as dark as it had when we left the house.

Chapter 2
Ready to Go

The last two weeks had been manic. Dad got the details for the new job through quite quickly by e-mail, but the new company wanted him to start as soon as possible. Mum and dad held a family meeting and told us that the house was already up for sale and we would be moving out in three days. Of course, that would be just the start of it. Mum couldn't fly you see. She had had an operation a few months before and there was still a chance that flying could cause a blood clot, which would be very bad news, even fatal. Which meant, we had to go by boat. Well... a ship obviously. It was 3,600 miles from Windsor to Canada and would take about ten days to get there.

The movers were to arrive the following day and EVERYTHING in the house was being packed up in crates. Sal and I were still going to school till the end of Thursday; mainly to keep us from being under mum and the movers' feet. At least it gave me more time with my friends before we left. When we got home from school, mum told Sal and I to sort out all our things and decide what we wanted to take with us and what could be got rid of. I thought it was going to be really hard as at first I was determined to take everything, however, as I got sorting, I began to think about the move and how it was going to be a complete fresh start. And what do you know? Suddenly I didn't want to take all my stuff. It all represented my life there in Britain, and that was about to end. I was going to start a new life and I wanted to start it fresh and clean. I would leave all my stuff behind; the games, the football stickers, my models, everything. All I would take would be my books and after I had packed, I just had one small box and that was it. Mum was amazed but didn't argue. Everything else was going to a car boot sale our friends were having after we had gone.

I went on the internet and did some research on where we were going in Canada. Wow! The place we were going to was in Nova Scotia, which is on the East coast of North America and just above the United States. It looked pretty isolated but the houses were all wood and painted crazy colours. You could tell fishing was big business there from the number of fishing boats. They were deep sea trawlers that go far out into the Atlantic Ocean. Man! It was just so different from there in Windsor. The nearest village was over fifteen miles away; you'd pass through seven or eight villages in that distance around here. Canada was just so big, there were vast, blank spaces on the map with nothing in them, well, I mean, there must be something, but not humans or anything manmade. The place looked kind of cool though and I was beginning to feel a bit excited about the new start.

By the 18th November I was shattered. The removal company finished packing that morning and when they left, the house was completely empty. Mum, dad, Sal and I were sitting on the floor in the living room. Sal wasn't happy but at least she hadn't been crying for the last week. She told me the night before that she had broken up with her boyfriend. He had done it; said it wasn't worth it with her moving so far away and up and left her there and then. Sal seemed to have taken it pretty well, no histrionics - I think she knew it was going to happen and had prepared herself - though I saw what she had written on Facebook about him afterwards and it was pretty harsh. I didn't think any girls who read it were going to go near him... for a while anyway.

We each had a small suitcase with clothes, toiletries and odds and ends to keep ourselves entertained for ten days or so and at six we loaded the car and were ready to set off. My best mates John and Alex turned up to see me off and gave me a present. They told me not to open it until I got to Canada. There was a tear in my eye I can tell you as we loaded the car up. They waved me off as dad pulled away and my heartfelt bitter and full of regret once again at being ripped away from the life I'd known and loved. I lost sight of them as we tuned out of our road and we were well and truly on our way.

I was sitting in the hotel we were staying in that night. The ship was to sail at seven in the morning so dad drove all the way from Windsor to Cardiff without a stop. Four hours solid. I was busting for a wee but dad wouldn't stop. I literally jumped out of the car when we got to the hotel. It was an old Victorian town house with ten rooms and a small dining room. It was a bit grubby and run down but dad wanted a place near the docks so it would be easy to get to in the morning. If we missed the ship, that would be it for the job.

The bed was hard and there was a lot of noise as the hotel was on a busy road. I wasn't sure if I'd be able to sleep. The adventure would really begin in the morning.

Chapter 3
The Crossing

It was Friday 19th November and dark when dad woke me and a real struggle to get out of bed. By the time I was washed and dressed it was quarter past five in the morning. It really did feel like the middle of the night. And then mum told us that it was too early for breakfast at the hotel. Sal and I moaned like anything about that. So, tired, hungry and cold we loaded up the car again and set off for the docks. The harsh cries of seagulls signalled how close we were to the sea as the sky in the east lightened and dawn approached.

The docks were massive, with cranes towering high into the sky, stacks of lorry sized containers by the thousand and the gigantic container ships lined up along the quays loading or unloading. It looked like the place was busy all night long.

Dad had arranged for someone to meet us there and take the car away to be sold. Mum, dad, Sal and I were left standing on the quay next to the pathetic looking pile of our belongings. An officer came down the gangplank of the container ship we were going to be sailing on. It was medium sized apparently but still looked as long as two football pitches and as high as a modest tower block.   The officer took us on board and showed us our rooms.   Obviously this wasn't a cruise liner, it carried cargoes of containers around the world, but as well as the crew's quarters, it did have four cabins, just in case, as passengers were not unknown.   It had worked out just right for us for two reasons, first, dad wanted to travel with our container of furniture and other stuff so we arrived at the same time and weren't left weeks waiting for it to arrive; secondly, it was cheap.   And at the moment that was real important as the house hadn't sold yet and money had become very tight.

Cabins they might have been, luxurious they surely weren't.   The four cabins were deep down in the bowels of the ship; no portholes or carpet, just beds, cupboards and a sink.   The floor was red, painted metal and there was a constant hum from the engines that couldn't be far beneath our feet.   There was a communal bathroom at the end of the passage, but as we were the only passengers, that didn't really matter.   What I was most certainly not happy about was having to share a cabin with my sister, Sal.   That was seriously not funny!

We all stood on deck when the ship sailed at seven.   The 'Spirit of Neath' (that was the name of the ship) blew its horn loudly as we began to pull away from the quay.   We waved farewell to the land where we had all been born and grown up and Britain slowly dropped astern.   Before long the cliffs along the coast became indistinct and were eventually lost over the horizon. I'm pretty sure we all felt some sadness, but the great adventure had truly begun then and I felt more excitement than sadness.

You really get a sense of the size of an ocean when there are no other ships around and nothing from horizon to horizon but grey sea. The weather was good, though it was really cold and the sea was calm and flat. I walked around the cargo deck the first morning; there were literally hundreds of containers stacked nine or ten high. Each one was the size of the trailer on an articulated lorry and they towered high into the sky. One of the officers told me that if there was a really bad storm and the seas got particularly high, there was a chance of losing some of them over the side. Apparently it happened quite often. My fingers were crossed that it didn't happen to our container. I didn't know which it was but it must have been one of the last to be loaded as it only arrived the previous afternoon, same time as us, so it must have been near the top of one of the piles. I kept my fingers crossed for a long time in the hope it would guarantee us good weather!

So... it was five days at sea that morning, and the boredom had well and truly set in. I thought it would be great, seeing amazing creatures in the sea: whales, sharks, turtles, giant jellyfish, but I'd seen nothing. There were some dolphins in the distance which dad pointed out, and I thought I could see something through the binoculars... but I was not really sure.

I was so fed up that I was prepared to play with Sal, but she was in bed with sea sickness, as was mum unfortunately. They both looked sort of green and moaned a lot. Dad was looking after them, but he told me to clear off whilst he did it on his own because I kept making faces and going 'eeuugh!' every time they were sick, which seemed to be every few minutes.

The reason for the sea sickness was the weather. It had really turned. No more nice calm ocean; the sea was a vast expanse of rolling waves and the sky full of billowing clouds. The wind had picked up and you had to be careful or you could easily fall on the metal decking. Because of the waves, the ship rolled constantly. At that moment it was a slow sway from side to side as the ship rose on the top of one wave and dropped into the trough of the next. It was going to get worse though, the Captain told me. He was in the canteen for lunch and had taken to chatting to me if we were both there alone. He said the forecast showed a storm moving towards us from the coast of America. We couldn't avoid it as it was coming from the way we were going, if you see what I mean. 'It is going to get rough, Harry,' he said. 'A force ten storm, which means very high waves which will cause heavy impact on the ship and large amounts of spray that will severely reduce visibility.'

'Will we sink?' I asked; feeling quite alarmed.

'No,' he chuckled. 'The Spirit of Neath is built to stand much more punishment than this storm is going to serve up. But the cargo is always a worry up on deck and it will be unpleasant, especially if you're not used to life at sea.'

I felt better knowing the ship was not going to be in danger, but Sal and mum had been getting worse as the waves grew and the ship pitched ever more steeply. Dad had his hands full looking after them both. He could do little more than clean the sick buckets out every so often, wipe their brows with a damp cloth and try and get them to drink a little water if they could manage it. I sat with mum for a while but she really just wanted to be on her own. Dad told me not to worry and to go off and watch the storm.

I can't say I was sorry to get out of the cabins. The moaning and retching were horrible and they wouldn't feel better until the storm was past and the sea was calm again.

The storm was closing on us and the sea was now really rough with waves of ten metres or so. The wind had picked up and spray was being plucked from the foaming waves and hurled around, creating a mist that brought visibility down to a couple of hundred metres or so. I knew it was late now and dark outside but it would be fun to get out there and experience what a real storm was like in the open. I wanted to go down near the front of the ship - the 'bows' they're called apparently - and see if I could get a view of the storm as The Spirit of Neath headed straight into it. It would be safe enough if I was careful, I thought. There were rails all round the ship and I would keep a good hold of something solid at all times.

As I opened the door from the warmth and safety of the interior, it was almost ripped from my hands as the gale force wind took it. I was yanked forward into driving rain and as the door slammed back hard against the wall, my shoulder was jerked painfully. I pulled the hood of my bright, yellow parka tighter before using my whole body to shove the door shut again. As well as the rain which was falling in sheets, the air was filled with spray from the waves and it was impossible to see more than a hundred metres or so. I staggered forward in the howling wind, leaning my body forward to try and make headway against its incredible force. Reaching the handrail, I pulled myself tight against it and began to haul myself along, hand over hand.

I was starting to get frightened by the time I had gone no more than twenty metres. As the ship dropped into the trough of a wave, I was lifted almost bodily into the air before being pushed back to the deck as it rose up the next. I continued to haul myself along the railing, the rain pummelling my parka and the spray making we squint as sea water coursed down my face.

Eventually, I made it to the end of the stacked piles of containers, where I could see the bows as they plunged into the wave ahead. A huge sheet of spray erupted over the end of the ship as the bows dug into the wave before rearing up again. The water crashed over the deck ahead of me. If I had been standing there, I would have been washed overboard immediately. Fear engulfed me as I realised the enormity of my stupidity. Here I was, standing all alone, in the middle of the Atlantic Ocean in the middle of a serious storm. I had to get back. The storm had become much worse in just the ten minutes or so it had taken me to get here.

There was a grinding noise from somewhere above and as I peered into the gloom I saw two of the containers at the top of the stack moving; sliding out from the neatly ordered pile. The screech of metal on metal groaned over the noise of the storm. I looked on in horrified fascination as several more containers began to slide out from the stack as the ship leaned over to that side, tossed about like a toy by the unstoppable might of the angry sea. I held on for dear life as the ship keeled over further. The first container toppled from the top of the stack and, turning end over end, crashed over the side of the ship, passing almost directly over my head before smashing into the dark, heaving water. Moments later, at least a dozen more huge metal containers, each weighting many tonnes, overbalanced and spun like the blocks from a huge Jenga tower collapsing and crashed into the sea below. None of the containers had hit the ship, but that must have been by pure luck.

I stood rooted to the spot; drenched, shivering and too scared to move my hands from the guard rail. Suddenly, an arm grabbed me round the chest. With a cry of surprise, I turned to see one of the crewmen who worked on the ship. "Come on boy, we gotta get out of here or we'll be over the side," he shouted, to be heard over the wind. I just nodded and released my grip on the rail. The crewman had on a safety harness that was clipped to the rail and as he stumbled, step by step, back towards the safety of the accommodation section, I clung to him with all my might. At one point, as the ship heeled over again, more containers tumbled into the sea, but they were behind us now.

It took another agonising fifteen minutes to reach the shelter given by the mighty superstructure with the bridge perched high above. The crewman heaved the door open and pushed me inside.   I was safe and collapsed onto the hard metal floor.

Chapter 4
Arrival and Lost Luggage

To say I got a telling off for my stupidity in going out on deck in the storm would be an understatement. It was only after the storm had passed that I got it with both barrels though and that was twelve hours later. Everyone was too busy, ill or exhausted to deal with me.

The storm had got worse and we hadn't sunk but I was glad it was over by the middle of the next day. I was called to the bridge by the Captain who had a serious chat with me about how reckless I had been and that when one of the officers on the bridge had spotted me (which had been a miracle in itself in the dark and at the height of the storm) it had needed a volunteer to go out and rescue me. The Captain made it quite clear that the man had risked his life to save me. I could feel my face burning red with embarrassment. I respected the Captain and I had let him down as well as putting the seaman's life in danger. I apologised through tears that I just couldn't stop.

After that, dad was quite decent about it. He said he thought a dressing down from the Captain was enough. He said that he and mum had been beside themselves, thinking they had lost me for good. I was quite touched until Sal butted in with, "we were just planning the party to celebrate when you ruined it all and turned up alive."

"Sal!" dad said sternly; but it broke the tension and everything was alright after that. Now the storm had broken, mum and Sal had recovered from their sea-sickness and were up and about again. Mum had cleaned the cabins and there was nothing to do but mope around. We were almost there though. We would be docking at Halifax, Nova Scotia, Canada, at 0700 hours the next morning and we were all excited.

Our suitcases were all packed that night and we were up at 5:00 a.m. standing on deck peering into the distance to get our first glimpse of North America. Sal spotted it first; just a faint smudge on the horizon that grew until land could be seen quite clearly and ran right and left as far as the eye could see.

Halifax is the capital of Nova Scotia and is found at the end of a long inlet. As The Spirit of Neath sailed along this wide channel, I could see hills and woodland lining the shore. It looked quite wild with not many buildings; until we passed what dad said was called McNabs Island in the centre of the inlet. From there on the city started and boy, it looked so modern and clean. The air was clear and bright and the city looked like a mini New York; dozens of tall office blocks and piers stretching into the inlet.

There were other ships and boats of all sizes sailing in various directions. Some of the buildings looked quite old but quaint and were painted bright pastel colours whilst others looked hyper-modern, almost space age.

The Spirit of Neath sounded its horn long and hard and within half an hour, the cargo ship was moored by a long, wide pier lined with cranes and warehouses.

As we were gathering at the gangway to disembark, I heard the Captain's voice calling me. He beckoned me over to him and squatted down on his haunches, "I enjoyed our little chats," he said. "And I've got a little something for you. I know you were eager to see some wildlife on the voyage over and there wasn't much to see, but now you're here, you're in for a bit of a treat. I'd like you to have this." With that he took something out of his pocket and looped a necklace over my head. There was something dangling from the necklace and he held it firmly in one hand. "I found this at an old whaling station up in the arctic circle one time. It's the tip of a harpoon they used to use to kill the whales. When they used to get up close and personal to the giant beasts and throw the harpoons like spears. It reminded me of what we did, driving those beautiful creatures to the edge of extinction. I want you to have it to remind you." The Captain stood, tousled my hair and was gone. I held the iron harpoon-tip up in one hand; it was six or seven centimetres across; dark, pitted and heavy. I tucked it inside my shirt and ran down the gangway to where my family were already standing on Canadian soil for the first time.

We all felt lost in this new, strange country I know. We made our way to customs where our passports and dad's work permits were checked. Soon after, we left the docks and found ourselves a taxi. We were booked into a local hotel for the night as we had to wait for the container with all our belongings to be unloaded. Then, we would follow it for the short journey to Peggy's Cove, the village we would live in. I marvelled at how tidy and clean Halifax was. The streets were wide and everything looked newly painted. The hotel was just a guest house with a handful of rooms. The landlady was round and friendly, chatting away as she showed us our room.

I still couldn't believe we were here. It seemed more like a holiday than the next step in our lives; a dream almost.

If it was a dream, it was well and truly shattered when at about 6:00 p.m. that evening the shipping company rang with the news that after they had taken an inventory of the cargo, it was discovered that our container of belongings had been one of those that was lost overboard in the storm.

Mum and Sal cried a lot; everything that was to remind us of home was gone.

Everything we needed to fill our new home here was gone.

There was a cloud over us as we went to sleep that night; a sense that we had made a terrible mistake coming all this way; that the whole dream was doomed to failure.

Chapter 5
Our New Home

I don't know if you have ever been in a position where you have had nothing at all; no home, no furniture, no clothes, no personal belongings? Well, I can tell you... it sucks. Admittedly we had the few clothes in our suitcases and a handful of personal things in our rucksacks but that was about it. Sal had been in tears all night and mum looked ten years older. Dad put on a brave face and told us we could buy everything from new; that it would be a real fresh start. It didn't help much. It wasn't so bad for me as I hadn't packed much to bring anyway; but I felt for them.

The next morning, dad hired a car. It was huge; more like a boat; light brown with an enormous boot and a rear door that swung out to the side instead of up. With our suitcases and rucksacks in, the boot was still only half full. As we drove out of Halifax, I looked at the people and buildings; in many ways they were the same as back home but in others they really were completely different. It took a while to get used to driving on the other side of the road as well. I thought we were about to crash into other cars heading our way for the first ten miles. After that, I was completely absorbed looking at the scenery. It was like looking at a movie set; the road hugging the coast and all the way the Atlantic glittering off to the left with smooth, bare rock and low cliffs taking the impact of the gentle waves of the currently calm ocean. To the right, we wound up and down hills covered in grass and every so often caught glimpses of vast woodlands beyond. I glimpsed a moose standing alone on one of the hills and it looked magnificent; proudly standing on the ridge with its front hooves planted wide and its mighty head thrust forward, the antlers spread out above it like a huge crown. I craned my neck round as the hill fell behind us; the moose remaining there proudly, for all the world like an ancient king surveying his vast kingdom.

It took half an hour before the first house came into sight. The feeling of how isolated this little community we were to become a part of was had started to dawn on me as the miles of rock and woodland had passed by. This first house was more of a hut really; single storey, one window and a door, pale blue, stained paint flaking from the old wooden planks. The road wound round another hillside and there was Peggy's Cove, laid out before us. The fifty or so houses were wooden and painted. Smartly kept, they had tiled roofs and small yards with wire fences round. Many of the houses seemed to be clinging to the bare rock that extended out beyond the tiny village and finally curled round creating a bay that several houses lined. Out on the tip of this peninsula there sat the squat octagonal tower of a lighthouse. I suppose it rose about ten metres in the air, the whitewashed stone set off by the red lamp room perched on top. It looked at once beautiful and strangely lonely at the same time.

There were several fishing boats along the quay but I couldn't see any people at all. Which of these strange wooden houses would be our new home, I wondered. Dad drove slowly down the road and into the village. It would be ridiculous to call it a main street as it only passed a couple of the houses. Most of the houses were set back with dirt tracks leading down to the road. Finally, dad pulled up at what looked like a store. It had children's fishing nets and other touristy knick-knacks piled in barrels beside the door. We all got out to stretch our legs for a minute. There was a strong breeze coming off the ocean and the smell of salt and seaweed was thrilling.

'Morning ya'll. Can I be helping you folks?' said a large woman in a long dress and apron, who had come out of the shop as we were moaning to each other. Her voice was like treacle and rich in the Canadian accent.

'Very possibly, I hope,' said dad. 'The name's Medhurst, Charlie Medhurst.' He reached out his hand and the woman shook it warmly in her bear like paw.

'Pleased to meet'cha Charlie. I'm Martha but most people just call me Ma. I recon I know who you are with that English accent. You the boat man? We been expectin' ya for a week past.'

'Yes that's me,' said dad. 'I'm afraid it's been a bit of a nightmare trying to arrange travel details. This is my wife Gill and my children Sal and Harry.'

We stepped forward one at a time and shook hands with this enormous, friendly woman.

'We're looking for the house that has been rented for us,' said mum. The company said that if we called at the store we could get the key.'

'And sure that's right,' the woman called Ma said. 'Hold on just a tic and I'll get 'em.' She disappeared inside the dark interior of the store from which the delicious smell of baking cookies wafted and returned moments later. Grasped in her hand was an iron ring about the size of a small saucer and hanging from it were several keys, each of which must have been ten or twelve centimetres long. As she handed them over, I couldn't help thinking they looked more like the keys to a medieval castle than a house.

'Why thank you,' said dad, uncertainly eyeing the keys. 'You couldn't point us in the right direction could you?'

'Why bless you,' said Ma chortling to herself, 'its right over there.' Ma pointed vaguely in the direction of the Atlantic, which didn't seem much help.

'I'm sorry to be such a nuisance, but could you be a little more specific,' said dad in a slightly exasperated voice.

Ma looked bemused before she replied, 'why right over there. Ain't you folks seen a lighthouse before?'

So there it was. As the whole family Medhurst stood, mouths open, staring at the lighthouse standing on the peninsula, the full extent of our new beginning in Canada finally sank in to each of us. Dad, I knew, would be panicking about what Mum thought; mum would be horrified at the thought of a dirty old lighthouse standing all alone and away from any friendly faces; Sal's tears would be for the lack of boys, nightlife and... Boys, whilst the grin on my face was because this was the real adventure I had hoped it might be. I was over the moon and when I was sitting back in the car ready to go, the rest of the family were still looking like startled rabbits.

The car pulled away from Ma's store shortly after with an additional box of fresh groceries Ma had put together to see us through till we were settled in.

Silence reigned on the short drive to the light house. There was a right turn as the single road through Peggy's Cove left the last house and this - little more than a dirt track - wound out behind the few houses and out along the peninsula. The track was basically just bare rock; flattish and about three metres across before the rock became boulders and slopped off to the sides, down to the water's edge. On the left was the Atlantic Ocean and on the right the quiet water of the small bay that protected Peggy's Cove and her boats from the worst the great ocean could throw at them.

It was only about a hundred and fifty metres to the lighthouse, but it might have been a hundred and fifty miles as we climbed out of the car. There was a rough car park that would fit maybe ten cars at a pinch on the tip of the peninsula, where the rocky outcrop was much bigger and rose to about five metres with the lighthouse perched above us. There were some small bushes here and there and tough, coarse grass growing in cracks between the rocks. A path with rough steps wound up the side of the grey stone and we hauled our meagre bits of luggage up the track. Mum and dad were stony faced and Sal was grumbling to herself as she stumbled along. Only I had a wide grin on my face, though I kept it hidden by keeping my head down. At last we reached the base of the lighthouse which towered above us and dad pulled the ancient keys Ma had given him from his pocket. The door was white and solidly built. The paint looked fresh and the walls of the tower that curved away to each side looked well maintained as well. The key turned and with the most eerie creak you could imagine, the door swung open. As we walked in, I looked around in wonder. It was like an

33

Aladdin's cave of treasures from the sea. The adventure really had begun.

Chapter 6
Making New Friends

The lighthouse was not very big. The ground floor was one room with a kitchenette area at one side and a living area with a sofa and two armchairs, all threadbare and sitting on top of an old, frayed Persian rug. The walls were whitewashed and octagonal, like the outside of the building. There were shelves on the walls and these, along with every windowsill and nail in the wall were adorned with bric-a-brac from the sea; lanterns, bells, ropes, nets, shells, even a ships wheel hung above the little stove in the small fireplace. A spiral staircase stood in one corner and wound up into the second floor, where there was a double bedroom and a tiny bathroom that contained a toiled, steel hand-basin and a shower cubicle. The black, iron spiral stairs continued up to the final floor that was entirely bare apart from two small, metal framed beds complete with thin, lumpy mattresses. Whilst this was the last of the living space, the stairs continued up into the lamp room. I was the first to race up the stairs, push up the trapdoor and squeeze through. Panting, I stood and looked around. The giant lamp filled most of the space, but as I walked round, what really caught my attention was the view. All around I could see for mile after mile; to landward, past the little fishing village of Peggy's Cove and the hills, scrubland and forests beyond, whilst the bare, rocky coastline stretched away on either side and finally, the great Atlantic Ocean, stretching for thousands of miles. Somewhere out there was the home I had left; just across the water but oh so far away. For a moment I felt utter loneliness and isolation from all I had ever known, but beneath that was a joy at being here. And, as if to help raise my spirits; a few hundred metres out, a whale suddenly rose from the sea and crashed back; raising a huge plume of white water. I nearly clapped my hands at the sight and I couldn't stop the smile that split my face.

After we had looked the place over, it was decided that Sal and I would share the top floor room. Neither of us was very pleased about this and Sal almost screamed the place down about needing privacy at her age. I could see her point... I didn't want to share with her either; all that make-up and perfume lying all over the place. I said I would sleep on the sofa downstairs if no-one objected... they didn't, so that's where I slept the first night after everyone else had gone to bed. We had skipped lunch after a big breakfast at the hotel in Halifax, so when we had unpacked the few things we still had and gone for a walk around the headland, mum made a stew from the groceries Ma had prepared for us. It must have been the fresh

Canadian air but by seven in the evening, none of us could keep our eyes open. Mum, dad and Sal went off to their beds in the upper rooms of the lighthouse whilst I got out a duvet and slung it over the sofa. Before I turned in I felt like taking a look at the view outside at night. I slipped on my coat, gloves and hat and quietly crept through the door.

It was bitterly cold outside and the clouds and rocky landscape were bathed in a silvery light from the bright, full moon. And then, the great light above me swung round and a beam of hot, yellow light stabbed out into the distance. The light was obviously controlled automatically, on some sort of timer. For a few moments the peninsula and village were lit almost as brightly as in the middle of the day and then the beam was gone, circling round as it sent its gaze out over the wide, dark Atlantic Ocean. It was almost magical and I realised I had been holding my breath. I breathed again and walked down the track to the parking area, the light from the lighthouse passing over me every ten seconds or so as the great light slowly rotated. I sat on a rock for a few minutes, looking over the small bay towards the handful of houses that made up Peggy's Cove; it was still early and there were many lights on in the windows of the old-fashioned wooden houses, smoke curled from the chimneys of most as the inhabitants did their best to keep the cold at bay. There was a sudden

37

movement off to the right, away from the village and hard to see in the darkness, but there was a definite movement, some animal I was sure. A sliver off fear ran down my spine as I had read about some of the wild animals found in Canada. But my curiosity held me there, peering into the darkness, trying to make out exactly what it was. The moon came out from behind a cloud and I could see a creature on four legs, a long body and a tail. It moved slowly and cautiously as though it was hunting. What could it be? A wolf? Surely I had read there were no wolves in Nova Scotia, hadn't I? It looked like a wolf though. The creature must have been about a hundred metres away near the foot of the peninsula where you turned to come up to the lighthouse. I couldn't be sure. I stood up to get a better look and instantly the creature turned its head and seemed to stare straight at me. I was quite spooked at that. A hundred metres might seem quite a distance but I was about thirty metres from the lighthouse now. If it charged at me, would I be fast enough to get back to safety first? I decided not to wait and find out, but turned and ran back up the track and only stopped when I had closed the great, solid wooden door of the lighthouse behind me.

I slipped out of my clothes and climbed beneath the duvet on the sofa. The room was warm from the dying embers of the fire in the wood burner and I soon slipped into a deep sleep, where a pack of wild wolves chased me through a forest.

I was awoken by the smell of pancakes cooking and quickly dressed as mum was about to serve up and dad came down dressed in his work suit. He was going to have to start work today and it was a long run back into Halifax. Sal was still in bed, so we ate her pancakes as well, smothered in maple syrup and with a dollop of vanilla ice-cream. That was a breakfast I could get used to. It had been decided that as it was already the first of December and the schools broke up on the twentieth, I would start school after Christmas, so I had just over a month of holiday. I had great plans to explore, though I was a bit concerned about making friends. I had been upbeat about making a new set of friends in Halifax when I saw the size of it, but out here in Peggy's Cove, how many children would there be? And the journey to school, which would be back in Halifax, would take an age. I was going to have real long school days and any friends I made there, when would I ever get to see them outside of school when I lived so far away?

Dad left for work in the boat-like car at about quarter past seven, and as Sal had still not made an appearance I decided to take a look round the new neighbourhood. It was bitterly cold outside so I wrapped up warm and added gloves, scarf and hat to my outfit. As I closed the door, my breath billowed around me like smoke. It only took five minutes to walk down to the parking lot and out along the peninsula back to Peggy's Cove itself. There were a few old men down at the dockside readying their boats for sea, piles of woven lobster traps covered much of the quay and fishing nets hung over wooden frames, drying.

As I walked through the widely spaced houses I saw that the store was open and just back from the quay was a restaurant called The Sou' Wester; closed now but the menu of fresh fish looked mouth-watering and the views across to the Atlantic were amazing.

As I ambled along the road, I saw a yellow bus drive into the village. It turned around at the end of the street and passed me as I walked down to Ma's store. I realised it was the school bus and a dozen faces were pressed to the glass, staring at me. The bus pulled up at a bus-stop just along the street and I saw three youngsters in school uniforms climb aboard. Two looked like older boys and the third, a girl who I guessed to be about my age. As I watched them clamber aboard the bus, the girl turned in my direction and stared straight at me. Her red stripped hat hid much of her face, but I was aware of two bright eyes regarding me; there was a sadness about that gaze, but also the hint of a smile on her small face, cheeks red in the biting cold. And then she turned and climbed onto the bus, which trundled off with a roar of diesel smoke from the exhaust. I realised I had been holding my breath for some time and let it out, panting for a few moments. So those would be my potential friends when I started school after Christmas; well the older boys might be a laugh, if they were willing to knock around with a little runt like me; the girl, I just didn't think about; as if I would hang out with a girl.

There was no point thinking about school and new friends at the moment as they were weeks and miles away. I turned my thoughts back to investigating Peggy's Cove. Where I stood at roughly the centre of the village, I could see every house. I ambled down towards the quay and crossed the road towards the store. It was about half past seven and I could hear bright cheery country music playing through the door of Ma's shop. Hands thrust deep in my pockets; I walked up the wooden steps and pushed open the screen door. There was once again the mouth-watering smell of baking and the store was one large room with a central rack of groceries and shelving along both sides holding more stuff for sale. Mostly it was food but there was a glass cabinet of knives and a magazine shelf and the far end of the store was filled with the counter and large double doors into a back room. Around the top of the walls were all kinds of things like moose antlers, fishing nets, guns, bear traps and even skis, hung on display. It was a wonderful place and warm as well. Ma stepped out from the back room having heard the bell ring as I had entered. 'Hi there young un,' she said, 'you want a piece of pie?'

'I'd love one,' I said, my mouth watering.

'Just pull up a stool then,' said Ma, disappearing into the back again. As I reached the counter, I realised it was more like a bar with stools and a cake stand with the most amazing cake selection you could imagine. I plonked myself on one of the stools, elbows on the counter and waited. Ma wasn't long in returning, a steaming slice of cake and a mound of ice-cream on a plate in her huge hand.

'That's apple and cinnamon cake. Let me know if you like it,' she said placing the plate in front of me along with a spoon.

'It's amazing,' I said through the first mouthful, crumbs falling onto the counter. It was a really great cake; moist and bursting with flavour. As I scrapped the last sticky crumbs from the plate it was all I could do to stop myself licking it. 'Oh,' I said suddenly, 'I haven't got any money with me.'

Ma laughed heartily, 'don't you worry 'bout that, if I offers you sumthin', it's for free. So, how you settling into the lighthouse? Kinda lonely I guess if you all aren't used to it. You folks come from a city back home?'

'Yes,' I said. 'Well... a big town, but close to London so it's very busy and noisy.'

'Yep, recon this will be a mighty big change. Not starting school yet?' she asked.

'After Christmas. Dad said I could have a few weeks to settle in first. But I'm not sure what I'll do; there don't seem to be any kids my age around and it's getting really cold,' I said, suddenly realising how difficult it was going to be to fill my time from then until Christmas.

'You like animals?' asked Ma, hands on her hips.

'Yes,' I said cautiously.

'Well, you could do worse than dropping in on ol' Gabe and Jen at The Sanctuary just round the Cove on Lobster Lane.'

'What's The Sanctuary?' I asked, intrigued.

'I'll let you find that out for yourself if you decide to pay 'em a visit. Now, time for you to scoot young un.' Ma walked round the counter and shooed me out of the store. 'Don't be a stranger,' she called as I walked off.

'I won't,' I called back, waving over my shoulder. 'And thanks for the cake.'

I wandered around for a couple of hours, just looking at things in the cove, but I was soon getting cold in the rising breeze coming in off the Atlantic. I headed home and was soon sitting in front of the wood burner with a mug of sweet tea in my hands. The rest of the day I

43

spent reading one of the two books I had brought along in my rucksack, but by six, I was bored and ready for supper. Mum said dad would be home about seven and Sal, who had been in her room all day, finally came down and lounged on the sofa beside me.

'I'm starting school tomorrow,' she said. 'I've got to get out of here and mix with some people my own age. Why don't you do the same?' she asked. 'You must be bored to tears here, in the middle of nowhere and no other children to play with.'

'Maybe... I don't know yet. I'll leave it a couple more days then decide.'

The door rattled as the handle was turned and it swung inwards to reveal dad, wrapped in coat and scarf and looking tired. Mum rushed up and hugged him tightly. 'How was your first day dear?' she asked, the concern clear in her voice.

'Well... it was an experience, that's for sure,' said dad. 'The drive's not too bad; I was in Halifax inside fifty minutes. The company is down at the docks and it's a small business in a wooden boathouse. Just fifteen people work there and I had a broken desk in one corner. They were over the moon to see me; been without a design engineer for months. I'd say it has a nice family feel to it and they've set me to design their next small fishing trawler. I think I'm going to like it there darling.' A smile cracked dad's face and he whirled mum around, with her shrieking as he tried to kiss her.

'Let's go out for dinner to celebrate,' said mum breathlessly when dad had finally let her go.

'That's a fine idea,' said dad. 'But where should we go around here?'

'How about The Sou' Wester in Peggy's Cove?' I said. 'I saw it this morning. The fresh fish on the menu looked great.'

'That sounds perfect,' said dad.

An hour later, we were all dressed up in the best clothes we had and were walking along the peninsula towards Peggy's Cove. When we arrived, the restaurant was lit by bright neon lights around the big, feature window. The sound of music could be heard from inside. As dad opened the door the smell of seafood filled our noses. There was a bar area over towards the back and a dozen or so tables in front. Three of the tables were occupied by two couples and a group of six adults. A tall, wiry man waved from the bar and came over. 'Hi ya'll, I'm betting you're the British folks, taken up in the old lighthouse eh? Heard all about you.' He reached out and shook each of our hands warmly. 'The name's Sandy, Sandy Banks. I'm the owner of The Sou' Wester. You're mighty welcome and this meal's on the house.'

Dad tried to argue, but Mr Banks, though he insisted on being called Sandy, would not hear of it. We were seated near the window with a lovely view of the Atlantic Ocean with the lights of fishing boats on their way back to shore twinkling in the distance. The food was simply delicious. We all loved seafood and this was some of the freshest I had ever eaten; mussels to start then lobster (Sandy insisted) followed by cheesecake.

As we were having coffee, I glanced out of the window and my eye was caught by a movement out towards the now deserted quay. I looked more carefully and the hairs stood up on the back of my neck as I recognised the same low shape and loping stride of the beast I had seen the night before at the base of the peninsula. The creature; dog, wolf, whatever it was, kept disappearing behind lobster pots and sheds, but I was sure it was the same animal. It appeared once again from behind a low building and suddenly stopped, the head turning and I felt my heart turn to ice as I sensed that it was staring at me. How could it know I was in here? It couldn't, but there it was in the dark and shadows of the night, watching me. The ice that had gripped my heart now turned to beads of hot sweat standing out on my forehead. Quickly, I turned back to the conversation between mum and Sal. 'You all right son? You look like you've just seen a ghost,' said dad.

'I'm fine,' I croaked, trying hard not to turn and look at the creature outside.

I think you'll recognise the next bit, because it's where I began the whole story. If you read it again, all I can say is that it was the real beginning of my adventure, although I still didn't know it.

It was gone ten thirty when we thanked Sandy, made our farewells and started on the walk back to the lighthouse. There was a frost already forming on the windscreens of the few cars parked in the main street and the sky was clear; millions of stars twinkling brightly like fairy dust thrown into the air. We walked briskly, our full stomachs complaining but keen to get back into the warmth of the lighthouse. There was no sign of the wolf now and I began to relax.

As soon as we got in, mum, dad and Sal went up to bed. Dad wanted an early night after his first day in the new job and Sal said she was bored. I sat on the sofa and tried to read for a while. I could hear footsteps upstairs and sounds of people using the bathroom. The book felt heavy in my hands and I just couldn't get into the story. I felt like skimming some stones across the Atlantic and hurriedly got back into my warm coat and scarf. There was a slight breeze outside and the frost was becoming thicker. I clambered over the rocks on the seaward side of the peninsula and found myself on a sloping boulder that ran into the water, the waves gently lapping at the white granite. I scouted around and soon found three or four flattish stones, ideal for skimming. Planting my feet wide, I heaved the first out into the Atlantic Ocean. It dipped quickly and sank without a trace. Disappointed, I took hold of a second stone and as I drew my arm back, there was a sound behind me. Glancing round, my eyes widened in horror as there above me, on the rocks and not more than ten metres away was the wolf; for a wolf it must surely have been, crouched on its haunches, teeth barred and ears laid back. Without thinking, I took a step back and the frost that had, without me realising, formed on the white stone took my feet from beneath me. I fell backwards and was instantly engulfed by the icy sea. My head went under and I spluttered for breath. The salt-water burned my nose and I coughed, arms flailing, trying to regain my feet. For a brief second my feet brushed against the boulder but then slipped away. Terror enveloped me as the water soaked my thick parka and its weight began to drag me down. Horrified, I realised I was about to be pulled down and drowned. I gasped a last breath before the ice-cold water closed over my head.

There was a tugging at my wrist. Something had grabbed the sleeve of my waterlogged parka and was pulling me. My feet kicked hard as I sought to push myself upwards, towards the person who was trying to save my life. Roughly, in jerking pulls, my shivering body was yanked from the sea; inch by inch, my arm stretched out above my head and my back against the rock I was dragged to safety. At last I lay gasping and spluttering, shaking uncontrollably in the icy coldness of the Canadian night.

At last, I looked up to see who my saviour was. My gaze took in the sight of the huge wolf, standing there; his head looming over me. The great beast suddenly threw back its head and began to howl; long haunting bellows that rent the night. I fought to get to my feet but my limbs wouldn't respond. The cold had drained the life from them and I knew with a sickening certainty that although I had survived the clutches of the sea, it would only be minutes before the cold finished the job. My body was rapidly losing the last of the heat it contained. The wolf continued to howl until suddenly, there was a light, flashing from side to side above and behind me and then a voice calling, 'Harry! Harry! Where are you son?'

I worked my lips, but no sound would come. At the sound of the voice the wolves head, which still loomed over me tilted down for a moment and dark eyes regarded me solemnly; and then it was gone; it vanished as if it had never been there.

'Thank God! Thank God!' the voice continued. I felt arms grab me and I was hauled up and over a shoulder. 'I've got you son. You'll be alright now.' And I knew I would.

Chapter 7
The Beast

I was in bed for two days. The doctor, who had to drive over from Indian Harbour, another village a few miles along the coast said I was lucky to be alive and wouldn't have been if I had been in the water for even another minute. I had a temperature and had to be wrapped in towels and put right in front of the stove when dad first carried me in. Now I just had a headache. Mum and dad were sceptical when I told them about the wolf; Sal actually laughed. They thought it was a figment of my imagination and that I had actually pulled myself out of the sea. Dad couldn't explain the howling that had brought him downstairs to investigate, realise I was missing and come rushing to find me. He had to admit that it had sounded like an animal but he had seen no sign of it.

It was Monday morning before I was allowed up and about; I was getting cabin fever with no TV or computer. After dad had gone to work I eventually annoyed mum enough with my constant nagging for her to relent and let me go out.

It was another cold day and the wind was blowing strongly from the west. Thick black clouds hurried across the sky as I walked down the peninsula towards Peggy's Cove. With my hands thrust deep into my pockets I thought about the wolf like creature that had haunted me since we had arrived there. Whilst I was still scared at the thought of it, I knew that it had saved me; when I thought it was going to attack it had actually saved my life. I wanted to see it again.

I found myself passing Ma's store and skipped up the steps and into the now familiar interior. Ma was standing on a chair, reaching high to clean the top shelves. 'Hi Ma,' I called out.

'Hi there yourself,' she replied looking over at me. 'Nearly a right short visit to Canada you had if what I hear's true.'

'Yes,' I said feeling embarrassed. 'I nearly drowned.'

'It's a common enough way to die round these parts,' she said. 'Not a family round here that ain't lost someone out fishing. The sea's a foe y' can't beat in the end.'

'Are there wolves around here?' I asked.

'Wolves? No, no wolves around these parts for nye on a hundred years. Though there are always reports from holidaymakers, claiming they see'd some. But take it from me, there ain't none. Why you askin'?'

'Well...' I hesitated, not sure if my story would sound preposterous to Ma. 'I've seen one.'

'What? A wolf?' laughed Ma. 'Now I seriously doubt that. I don't know what you saw but it certainly weren't no wolf.'

Feeling my face burn with embarrassment at her laughter, I said, 'But it *was* a wolf. I've seen it a few times and it saved me when I slipped and fell in the sea.'

Ma wasn't laughing now. 'So, tell me just what you did see then.' she said.

'It was big,' I began. 'It has always been at night when I've seen it, but I would say it was black, or grey with fierce eyes and it certainly howled like a wolf. That's how my dad found me on the rocks below the lighthouse.'

Ma looked thoughtful, her brow creased in thought. 'Well... that's mighty strange. But that weren't no wolf. Sounds like ol' Fury; Zachary Arnoud's dog. He were a big ol' brute.'

I was instantly interested at these words. 'So is that what it was? This guy's dog then?'

'Sit down and I'll tell you about it. Want a slice of pie?' Ma climbed down from the stepladder and went behind the counter. I sat on a stool and looked hungrily at the apple pie Ma was just shoving in front of me. As I tucked in, she began. 'Zachary Arnoud was the last lighthouse keeper here in Peggy's Cove. He was a strange one; kept himself to himself out there, all alone except for his dog. It was a huge thing; a cross between a German Shepherd and I don't know what; certainly could have been wolf looking at him.

He came into town once in a while... for groceries mostly. Always had that dog with him; called him Fury and the creature wouldn't let no one touch him 'cept for ol' Zac. Never left his side that I ever see'd. Then ol' Zac uped an died; heart attack they said. That was three years ago now.

'They modernised the lighthouse and automated it so there was no need for another keeper. But his dog stayed around. Often see it in the distance. Ol' Fury must be getting on for bein' six or seven or so. Won't let anyone near him though. Must find his own food and sleep in the woods. Never seems to stray far from the lighthouse though, where he and his master lived.'

'So it's Fury who saved me!' I said excitedly.

'Certainly sounds that way,' said Ma, rubbing her chin thoughtfully. 'Don't sound like him though; like I said, he's never let anyone near him, so you'd be the first.'

I didn't see anything of the great half-dog half-wolf Fury on my way back to the lighthouse and mum wouldn't let me out that night after what had happened. It was the next day before I could have a proper look around. It was the seventh of December and there were decorations up in the houses of Peggy's Cove. Nothing extravagant as there weren't many kids. But it looked nice and as it had started snowing heavily the night before, there was a real Christmassy feel to the place. Not at the lighthouse though as we obviously had no decorations and money was really tight now, until dad picked up his first pay check.

Mum was feeling lonely and bored. She was stuck in the lighthouse all day and hadn't got to meet hardly anyone. I mentioned it to Ma and she said she would call by and invite her to a book club in the village. By lunch time that day Ma had already dropped by. Mum made her tea and by the time she left (about two hours later) mum was laughing and seemed really excited about going to this book club. Ma had even asked her if she would like to do some baking for the store and mum was already planning some of her best cakes to try out on the locals.

It was the morning of the ninth of December and there were four or five inches of snow on the ground. I told mum I was going for a walk along the coast; she looked worried and made me promise not to walk too close to the sea. So, off I set after a hearty breakfast. Walking along the peninsula, instead of turning left towards Peggy's Cove, I turned right to walk along the rocky shoreline where the trees began about twenty metres from the gently lapping Atlantic waves.

I had only been walking for ten minutes and the lighthouse was still large behind me when I came across an old boathouse. It was set back in the tree-line with old, rusty iron rails running down into the sea on a slope chiselled out of the white rock. It was clearly old and the boathouse unused with the wooden cladding rotten and falling away in places. The roof, lined with felt showed great jagged tears and a tree had fallen and partly caved in the far corner of the structure. At the front was a pair of large wooden doors, so dilapidated that I could not be sure of the original colour of the little paint that remained on them. One of the doors hung outward, a hinge having snapped. There was a gap through which only darkness could be seen. My sense of curiosity was aroused. I had nothing else to do but stroll aimlessly along the shore so I decided to see if there was anything interesting inside.

I had to bend and squeeze through the gap, but eventually I stood inside the boathouse. It was very dark with just a few beams of light shining through the holes in the roof. There was a strange smell that I couldn't quite place mixed with the distinct aroma of old engine oil. I edged my way in further, hands held out to stop myself bumping into anything. I had reached a timber pillar in the middle of the shed before I realised that the strange smell was wet fur. I had smelt it often on friends' dogs. I froze as I realised what that meant. A low growl sounded from the darkness ahead.

Slowly, breathing fast and shallow I backed up towards the dim light of the broken door behind me. I had barely taken two steps before I saw the outline of the great dog Fury dimly silhouetted in front of me. It was moving forward slowly. Was it stalking me? About to pounce and tear me to pieces? It continued to move towards me and eventually I could make out the eyes as dark pools, glinting slightly as the faint light from the door hit them. The huge dog was only a metre away now and the smell of wet fur much stronger. The dog was panting heavily. Shaking with fear, I reached my right hand out and instead of the agony of sharp teeth piercing my skin, I felt the rough rasp of Fury's tongue as it gently liked my fingers.

Chapter 8
Friends Come In Pairs

I sat on the rocks just above the sea and scratched the ear of Fury, who sat next to me. His fur was matted and full of burrs from the woods but he sat still as I gently teased each prickly lump from his body. Occasionally he turned his massive head and regarded me with those black eyes which were full of intelligence and sadness. I had realised immediately in the boathouse that he would not hurt me and now he was leaning his body against mine.

Eventually I knew it was time to get back home and as I reluctantly stood to say my goodbye and leave Fury to his isolated home, I was surprised when he stood as well. 'I've got to go,' I said. Fury cocked his head to one side and just looked at me. 'I'll come back tomorrow,' I promised. I turned and began to walk along the rocks towards Peggy's Cove. Looking back, I realised Fury was following me. I kept walking and he kept following, about five paces behind. I guessed he would eventually wander off on his own; but he didn't. Fury followed me all the way back to the lighthouse. When I reached the door he was still there. I opened it and hesitated, not sure what to do. Fury made the decision for me. He pushed past my legs and went straight through the door. When I closed the door, I saw my mum standing in the middle of the room, eyes wide in surprise and Fury curled up in the small space behind the spiral staircase. 'I think he's come to stay,' I said. Mum just looked at me with her mouth hanging open.

Dad, Mum, Sal and I sat round the dining table that evening. Fury had remained behind the staircase staring at me the whole time. I explained about Fury having belonged to the old lighthouse keeper and that he had lived on his own for years and how he had saved me when I fell in the Atlantic Ocean. They believed me now that they could see Fury themselves. 'It looks like he's adopted you,' dad said.

'Can he stay?' I asked.

'He could be dangerous,' said mum, glancing nervously in the dog's direction.

'Yeah, he looks nasty,' said Sal.

'Please,' I said.

'Well,' said dad doubtfully. 'He did save your life. We owe him a lot. Maybe we could give it a try for a few days. You'd have to look after him though.'

And that was that. Fury was part of the family... well, he wouldn't let anyone else touch him and growled if they tried, but with me he was quite different. He watched me all the time. At night he would come out, paw at the door and disappear into the night when it was opened. There would be a scratching at the door about three in the morning and I would get up, let him in and he would jump up onto the sofa and curl up next to me, his massive body keeping me extra warm.

I don't know why Fury chose me; I doubt I ever will. It was enough that he had and he became the friend I had not so far managed to make. During the day, he followed me everywhere. I walked into Peggy's Cove the day after he first stayed at the lighthouse and he followed me all the way, always five paces behind. I walked up the steps and into Ma's store. She nearly had a heart attack when she saw him and grabbed a broom. She held it up in both hands ready to strike, and Fury just looked at her. Eventually she calmed down and eyeing the huge dog warily, sat at the counter whilst I ate a slice of cherry pie. By the time I left, she was completely at ease with Fury being there... until she reached down to stroke his head; a deep growl came from inside the powerful beast and she quickly drew her hand back.

By then it was the fourteenth of December. There had not been any more snow but the ground was still covered and the temperature never rose above zero. Sal had been at school in Halifax for a couple of weeks and seemed much happier. She had already made friends and though none of them lived anywhere near Peggy's Cove, she kept in touch in the evenings and at weekends on her iphone. Dad promised to get a computer as soon as he could afford to so she could use the social networking sites.

I had Fury, and to be honest, until I started school after Christmas, he was enough... or so I thought. That all changed when the schools in Halifax broke up for the Christmas holidays. There weren't many kids in Peggy's Cove anyway but on the Friday morning, the day after the holiday had started I ran into the two teenage boys I had seen on the school bus. I walked up and said hi to them but they totally ignored me. Actually, one of them called out, 'Get lost Limey,' as I walked away, Fury following and casting unimpressed glances at the boys as we went. I wasn't too upset; they were a lot older than me; but I did feel more isolated at the taunt; more alone and cut off from the country I had known so well. As I glanced up I saw a small face at the upstairs window of a sorry looking, red painted house opposite where the boys were lounging. It watched me for a few seconds then disappeared. Bored, I decided to walk up to the main road that led into the village.

I hadn't gone more than a hundred metres before a girl's voice called out, 'Hey, wait up a minute.' I turned to see who it was and there was a girl, only part of her face visible through the opening in her parka hood. She stood, breathing heavily and must have been running to catch up with me. She undid her hood and pushed it back. I realised immediately that it was the girl I had seen on the school bus the day after we arrived. She had red hair curled up in a bun on her head, rosy cheeks and dark, piercing eyes. The girl took a step towards me and before I knew it, Fury had trotted forward and placed his great body between us. 'Hi ya Fury,' the girl said; reaching out her hand she chucked his ear playfully. I half expected Fury to go for the girl, but he didn't. He let her stroke his ear with his head slightly to one side. 'I'm Molly,' the girl said without looking up.

'I'm Harry,' I said feeling embarrassed.

'I seen ya from the school bus a while back,' she said. 'Been waiting for a chance to say hi.' She looked at me now, shyly.

'Well... it's nice to meet you,' I managed, feeling ridiculous.

'Don't suppose you're too keen on talking to me,' Molly said. 'Guess I'll be off then. Don't want to turn you any redder than you are now.' She stroked Fury's head one more time then turned and started walking back up the road.

'Don't go,' I called to her. I wasn't sure why I said that, apart from having realised she must have really rushed to get dressed and run out after me so quickly, just to introduce herself; and she had seen I had felt uncomfortable about her coming up to me. She turned and looked at me; her dark eyes staring straight into mine. 'I'm sorry,' I continued.

'It don't matter,' she said. 'There ain't no one else my age round here. Just thought it might be nice to get to know you.'

I felt even worse then, than I had before. 'Really,' I said, 'don't go. Do you fancy going for a bit of a walk with me and Fury here? I was going to walk up to the highway.'

Molly looked at me then at Fury. 'Okay then,' she said simply and walked back. All three of us started to amble up the road in silence.

It wasn't till we reached the fork where the Peggy's Cove turning joined the main road and both sat on a bench set back from the road with Fury lying on the snow covered ground between us that Molly said anything else, 'It very different here from where you come from in England?' she asked, staring up the road.

'In some ways, very different,' I said. 'In other ways - the most important ways - not very different at all. That doesn't stop me feeling homesick though. I miss my friends.'

Molly didn't say anything for a few moments. Eventually she said, 'Yeah, missing people's not nice. Reckon I can relate to that.'

'You can?' I asked, surprised. 'Did you come here from some other part of Canada then?'

She didn't respond to that; just sat there staring up the road. Eventually she said, 'Nope, I was born here, but I got to understand about missing people real well.'

Her reply puzzled me, but she didn't explain more and there was something in the air that told me she didn't want to talk about the subject any more. We just sat stroking Fury for a while. Eventually Molly stood up, 'I gotta get back. We're going shopping in Halifax for Christmas presents later.'

We both stood and began to trudge back towards Peggy's Cove. On the way she told me about some of the wildlife around those parts. She'd seen so many things, but it was her talk about killer whales, seals, dolphins and the sea otters that frequented the coast of Nova Scotia that really caught my imagination. When she stopped speaking I said, 'I can't believe you've seen all those. I wish I could. I've always wanted to see a killer whale.'

Molly stopped and looked at me, head slightly to one side, 'You don't have to wish no more,' she said. 'Not now you live here. You doing anything tomorrow morning?'

'No,' I said.

'Right, meet me outside the Sou' Wester at six thirty.'

'Six thirty?' I gasped. 'That's very early.'

'Got to be that early if you want to help out,' Molly said mysteriously.

'Where are we going?' I asked; my curiosity well and truly piqued.

Molly smiled, an open honest smile as she said, 'I'm going to take you to meet Gabe and Jen.'

'Who are they?' I asked, feeling sure I had heard those names before somewhere.

'Don't you mind who they are, just be outside the Sou' Wester at six thirty. Wrap up warm and make sure you're wearin' old clothes.' Molly punched me playfully on the arm. 'See you tomorrow Harry,' she said before turning and running up the steps and into her house.

I stood there for a minute thinking things over. In the space of a couple of days I had gone from being all alone in a strange country to having my own dog and girl friend. My mouth hung open, no, obviously I meant a friend who happened to be a girl. I felt a terrible redness rising up my neck until I thought my face must be about to burst into flame. Quickly, I shoved my hands deep in my pockets and, with Fury following five paces behind, made my way back to the lighthouse.

Chapter 9
The Sanctuary

That evening, when dad got home, there was a wide grin on his face. He waved a piece of paper in the air, 'My first pay-check,' he said. Mum rushed over and hugged him.

As it was Friday and the family Medhurst was flushed with cash for the first time in months; dad even took us into Halifax for a meal. It was my first time back there since we arrived and I have to say, it's an attractive city. Small, clean and full of open spaces; the streets and shop-fronts sparkled with Christmas lights, snowmen and Santas. It all looked quite magical.

The celebration was nothing extravagant, just Nandos, but that's what mum, Sal and I had all pleaded for. The restaurant was in the centre of the shopping district and we had a seat right in the window looking out at the milling crowds of shoppers, taking advantage of the late night shopping available this close to Christmas. It was well below zero and there was still snow on the ground even though it hadn't snowed for the last week.

When it came, the food was delicious; spicy and full of flavour. The restaurant was packed and the noise of the talking, laughing groups made it hard to hear anything my family said. As I sat there enjoying my food I looked out of the window. The crowds had thinned a good bit now and I saw a hunched man, hands thrust deep in his pockets marching along the opposite side of the street. Behind him a small girl ran awkwardly to keep up in boots that were too big. There was a crossing over a side street just ahead of the pair and the man stopped as the lights were red. The girl, with her head down didn't realise he had stopped and ran into the back of the old man. His reaction took me completely by surprise; he turned, his deeply lined face contorted in anger and shoved the girl hard in the shoulder. The girl fell backwards, sitting hard on the slushy pavement; her hood fell back and I gasped, suddenly realising why my eyes had been drawn to the pair. A mass of red hair was revealed along with the face of Molly. Even from that distance I could see that she was crying and rubbing her shoulder. The man didn't so much as glance at her, but turned and walked, in his hunched way across the street as the light turned green. Molly climbed unsteadily to her feet and ran in a stumbling lope after him. Moments later the pair were lost in the distance and mill of people. I put my knife and fork down; the food had suddenly turned to ash in my mouth. I looked around the table, where the love from the other three people there seeped through every word, gesture and look. There had been no love in what I had just seen happen to Molly. I was quiet and withdrawn for the rest of the meal and to amazed comments from the other Medhursts, passed on the dessert.

Fury was curled up on the sofa with me when my alarm went off at six the next morning. It was Saturday and the rest of the family would not be up for a couple of hours. Fury was already pawing at the door fifteen minutes later when I was washed and dressed. He rushed out, barking madly at nothing in particular, and I tried to 'shush,' him as quietly as I could. He completely ignored me and raced around the lighthouse and back round the other side. It was still dark and I took a torch to help see where I was going. I trudged steadily down towards Peggy's Cove; Fury running on his own, was out of sight in the darkness. I wondered about what I had seen the previous night; was that the normal sort of treatment Molly received from that man? And who was he exactly anyway? He hadn't looked anything like her, but I guessed he must have been her father.

It was six thirty five when I reached the Sou' Wester. Molly was leaning against the steps, 'You're late,' she said. She was dressed in old clothes with stains and tears in various places.

Where were we actually going? I wondered.

'Come on, we'll have to walk quickly now.'

Molly led the way out of Peggy's Cove. This time we headed west. I had never been along the coast on that side of the village before. Soon we had left the last house behind and were climbing a bluff that separated Peggy's Cove from the next stretch of coast. As we reached the top I could see for miles and cresting the summit of the bluff, another bay came into view; Cranberry Cove, Molly told me. This was much more open to the elements and the sea than Peggy's Cove. It was quite windy today and waves crashed against the stony shore. What caught my eye the most though was a big house half way round the bay. It was big, white and had a variety of big outbuildings. Was it a farm? We trudged down to the beach which was made up of smooth white and grey pebbles and made our way along it. Fury danced around in the breaking waves, snapping at the white foam.

It was bang on seven when we reached the house. Molly didn't knock on the door, but walked round the back of the house to the first of three big sheds. As she opened the door, a wave of noise struck me like a blow. Animal screeches of all kinds; it was like someone had turned the volume in a zoo up to full.

'What is this place?' I asked.

'This is The Sanctuary,' she said.

I felt no wiser. 'What's that then?'

'Gabe and Jen Munroe run it. They look after injured animals; release them back into the wild if they can. I come here to help out three, four times a week. Come on, let's find Jen,' she said and before I could ask anything else, she was marching in. I followed. Fury stood whining at the door, unwilling to go into the building.

The shed was more like a boarding kennels I had seen at home. About twenty metres long and five wide, a central passage ran the full length and there were brick cubicles along each side with metal mesh screens and doors to the front of each. The noise from these cubicles I quickly realised was mainly from seals that barked and honked at quite a pitch. The smell of fish was overpowering. The door of the end most cubicle was open and a figure clad in rubber galoshes and a boiler-suit backed out, spraying water from a hose inside. 'Jen!' shouted Molly.

The woman looked round. She was about thirty five with a pretty face and very slim, though she looked lost in the baggy clothes she wore. Her black hair was tied back and there was a broad smile on her face. 'Hi there Molly, glad to see you; got a lot of work to do.' She suddenly noticed me standing behind Molly. 'Who you got with you?' she asked.

'This is Harry,' said Molly.

'Pleased to meet you Harry,' said the woman. 'Going to lend a hand then?' she asked, her eyes smiled along with her face.

'Yes... yes, I suppose so,' I stuttered.

'That's great. Molly, you and Harry here can start in Shed 2, okay?'

'Sure thing,' said Molly and before I could complain, she had grabbed my arm and was dragging me towards the door we had come in through.

Shed 2 was at right angles to the previous shed but looked exactly the same, inside it was similar too, except that the cubicles were wider.

'This is where all the land mammals are kept,' Molly explained. 'Shed 1 is marine mammals, Shed 2 land mammals and Shed 3 is birds. Gabe and Jen run this place as a charity. They work hard and money is always tight but it's worthwhile to see these poor animals brought back to health and released back into the wild.'

I was amazed at the set-up here. Slowly, I walked along the cubicles; there were red squirrels, at least three porcupines, a beaver, a snowshoe hare and even a skunk in the furthest cubicle. Each had a label outside its kennel with the name of the breed and what was wrong with it. One of the porcupines had been hit by a car and the other had been stuck in someone's shed and nearly died of starvation; the skunk had been caught in an illegal hunting snare and found by a passer-by. All had tragic stories and most of them looked to be getting better. I could hardly take my eyes off of the animals, most of which I had never seen before. Mainly they were curled up at the back of the cubicle as far away from us as possible. One of the porcupines was curious and nudging his nose against the wire at the bottom of the door. I bent and stuck my finger through the wire to give its snout a stroke. I jumped back with a yelp as the creature bit me just below the nail of my index finger. It really hurt and I danced around, mouth open in a silent scream that wouldn't come. After a minute, the pain died down and I was able to examine the damaged digit; the skin was not broken, fortunately.

'They're wild animals,' said Molly severely. 'Generally they're terrified of you and we don't treat them like pets as they've got to be released back into the wild and a healthy respect for humans might just keep them alive in the future. If one bites you and it breaks the skin, it'll mean a tetanus shot. Come on, pick up the broom, I'll get the hose.'

For the next forty five minutes we moved along each cubicle and carefully, I swept out any droppings or leftover food whilst Molly sprayed the floor to ensure it was clean. After that we put down food and water for each patient; the food particular to that animal and taken from a fridge at the end of the shed. By the time we had finished, it was just before eight and Molly said it was time for breakfast.

She led me out of the shed and up to the back of the house. Molly didn't knock, just pushed the screen door open and we went in. The kitchen was organised chaos; the simple white painted kitchen units cluttered with mail, tools, and boxes of animal food and so on. There was an enormous bear of a man standing with his back to us, busy working at the giant range cooker in front of him. Molly pushed me forwards towards a bench at the pine table that was remarkably clear of clutter and laid for breakfast.

The huge man turned, he had a handsome face and kind eyes as well as arms that could have strangled a bull. A full beard suited his face and he was finished off by a pair of small wire glasses. In his hands he held a large plate of pancakes and a jug of maple syrup. Banging them down on the table, he plonked himself on the other bench and beckoned us to dig in.

I was ravenous and had finished two pancakes before Jen joined us. Gabe introduced himself and the story of Gabe and Jen Munroe and The Sanctuary at Cranberry Cove began to be told.

After meeting at university; both studying Veterinary Science, Gabe and Jen had joined Greenpeace, the environmental action group. They both had fierce beliefs in looking after the planet and reducing the damage we humans did to our home. They were involved in many protests, including very risky confrontations with Japanese whaling ships in an attempt to get a worldwide ban put in place. Eventually they left Greenpeace, wanting to develop more hands-on careers with the animals they loved. This took them to Alaska where they worked hard helping to preserve endangered species in the Arctic Circle. Then came the terrible Exxon Valdez disaster; a huge oil tanker ran aground off of Prince William Sound in Alaska. It was an area of outstanding natural beauty and the sea, coast and land around it was classed as a nature reserve because of the rare and varied wildlife found there. 120,000 cubic metres of oil gushed into the sea and the huge oil slick, when it reached the coast caused mayhem. Thousands upon thousands of sea birds, fish and mammals were coated in the sticky, suffocating crude oil. Most died, lying in the horrible thick layers of oil that lapped the beaches and covered the sand and rocks. As qualified veterinary surgeons, Gabe and Jen joined the rescue mission as soon as possible. Hundreds of volunteers flooded in to makeshift treatment stations where half-dead birds, otters, seals and many other species were brought in for the complicated cleaning process to begin. Painstaking washes with detergents, feeding and helping the creatures recuperate afterwards were non-stop. Many still died, but some survived. It was heart-breaking work that went on for weeks. By the end of the clean-up, both Gabe and Jen were utterly exhausted, but knew they had found their calling.

They married, moved to Canada and bought the house on Cranberry Cove. After they had set up The Cranberry Sanctuary charity, and some money began to come in, they had started the building work that over the years had become 'The Sanctuary' it was then. I loved the story and was nearly in tears when they talked of the terrible suffering of the animals during the Exxon Valdez oil spill.

'So, what do you think of it here Harry?' asked Gabe.

'It's great,' I said.

'Great enough for you to think about coming and helping out?' asked Jen.

I was taken aback at this, 'I... don't know,' I stammered. 'I'm not sure I'd be any good.'

'Well, Molly tells me you took to the basics like a duck to water this morning,' said Jen, her eyes twinkling.

I glanced at Molly; when had she had a chance to say anything about me to the Munroes?

'But... if you don't want to, that's fine,' said Jen, pursing her lips slightly.

'No... I do... I really do,' I said, only then realising how much I did want to work at The Sanctuary.

'That's great,' said Gabe. 'It's only voluntary work I'm afraid; no pay; but breakfast is thrown in, and supper, if you want to do an evening shift.'

And that was it. Without even really wanting one, I had a job, and I could feel a deep pleasure welling up inside me at the thought of working with all those wonderful wild animals. 'What about Fury?' I said suddenly. 'I don't know what he would be like with all these animals.'

Both Gabe and Jen smiled. 'No need to worry about that. Fury's no stranger here. And it's precisely because we heard that he had befriended you that you were invited along to The Sanctuary.

Amazed, I stared from Gabe, to Jen and then finally to Molly. It was Fury who had got me this job interview and fortunately I had passed.

Chapter 10
'Twas the Night before Christmas

The next week passed like a blur. As it was now the Christmas holidays and I wanted to fill my time in the absence of any friends yet - well, apart from Molly, I thought grudgingly to myself - I arrived at The Sanctuary every morning at seven. Sometimes I called for Molly on the way (she worked Monday, Wednesday, Friday and Saturday mornings), then walked over to Cranberry Cove with Fury trailing behind. I worked, cleaning out the cubicles and pens for an hour before meeting up with Gabe, Jen and Molly if she was there for breakfast at the great kitchen table. There were a few other volunteers who were much older and generally helped out during the day. I was blissfully happy. Most often I was in the bird shed with dozens of screeching terns, herring gulls, eider ducks and different types of geese. They were beautiful, graceful creatures, each with its own injury or illness to get over.

Sometimes I was in the mammals shed and that's where I most enjoyed spending my time. There was something special about the eyes and facial expressions that gave each one a personality and each had its own peculiarities, just like humans. The beavers and raccoons were incredibly naughty, the porcupine, shy and the striped skunk very short-tempered. We had a skunk in at the time and one day I was late with its food; it eyed me angrily then turned as I put the bowl down, lifted its tail and squirted me with the foulest smelling liquid imaginable. As I rubbed my eyes which were streaming, I began to gag and retch at the awful smell. It took me two days to get rid of the stench entirely and I wasn't allowed near anyone until it had finally gone (or to be more exact, everyone ran away from me). I treated any skunk with extreme respect after that and jumped out of my skin every time one twitched its tail.

There were other mammals as well; sometimes we had snowshoe hares, red foxes, mink, pine marten and red squirrels. The Sanctuary didn't take in any of the bigger mammals like moose, bears or deer, which were just too much of a handful for a small place like The Sanctuary. The last shed was reserved for marine animals like seals and turtles. It seemed that seals were constantly getting injured and there was a never ending stream of them arriving at The Sanctuary; cut up by boat propellers, attacked by sharks or killer whales or just plain poorly with some disease or virus. I liked them and their barking roars, but Dear Lord, they did stink of rotting fish; if one of them belched in your face (and

77

they regularly did) you could feel yourself turn green.

Mum and dad were really pleased I was helping at The Sanctuary. Sal just thought I was weird as I smelt of fish, or worse, most of the time. As I said, the days flashed past and before I knew it, it was Christmas Eve. Mum was going to cook Christmas dinner the next afternoon and we would all get together in front of the stove when everyone woke up and exchanged presents (just little ones this year, I had done all my shopping at Ma's store). At eight on Christmas Eve, when we were all sitting around the Monopoly board and fuming over our finances, we were startled when the phone rang. It hardly ever rang... well... who had our number? The phone had sat there, attached to the wall just next to the kitchenette, an old-fashioned style with a handset attached to the base with a coil of wire. Dad jumped up and answered the insistent ring. He spoke into the handset for a minute, glancing at me occasionally. Finally he put the handset down, 'Get your coat Harry,' he said in an urgent voice.

'What is it Charlie?' asked mum anxiously.

'That was Jen Munroe, from The Sanctuary,' he said. 'The place Harry helps out at. Apparently there's been an accident up on the highway past Indian Harbour. A car hit a bear or something. Her husband Gabe is down with food poisoning and she doesn't think she can deal with it herself. Wants Harry and me to help. I said yes.'

'Alright,' said mum doubtfully. 'Just be careful.'

In a minute or two we were both wrapped up and ready to go. 'Mrs Munroe is coming to pick us up in her truck,' said dad. 'I told her we'd walk down to the Sou' Wester and meet her there.'

We trudged quickly along the causeway; a thin drizzle had begun to fall, soaking everything and reducing visibility considerably. Fury as always was a few paces behind. Dad had wanted to leave him behind but he had shoved straight past the moment dad opened the door, almost as if he realised what he was thinking. The growl he made when dad tried to take him by the scruff and force him inside saw a rapid change of plan and Fury accompanied us. We had just reached the steps to the restaurant which was busy with loud revellers as the Toyota Hilux owned by the Munroes screeched up and skidded to a halt. The truck was battered but still a good runner. The bed of the truck, behind the double cab had been covered over and doors fitted to the back so it could hold injured animals. Dad scrambled into the back door and I jumped into the front passenger seat. Jen was already racing off out of Peggy's Cove by the time we had our seat belts done up. 'Thanks for coming,' she said in a strained voice. 'Gabe's in no fit state to move;

he's been throwing up since lunchtime. It's already been twenty minutes since the State Troopers called and that poor animal could be dead already.

'Where's the accident?' dad asked.

'Out on Highway 333; about ten kilometres from here. Just near The King Neptune Camp Site at Yankee Cove. 'It'll take us a good fifteen minutes to get there in this weather.' Not only was it raining harder now but there was the flash of lightning in the distance, followed by the dull rumble of thunder.

'Not exactly Christmas weather,' dad said dryly.

'Oh, it is in Nova Scotia,' said Jen.

'Was anybody injured in the crash?' I asked.

'Just cuts and bruises to the driver and his passenger according to the State Troopers. Probably a lot worse for the bear. Animals tend to come off somewhat worse in arguments with cars.'

The Toyota raced along Highway 333, water spraying off the road and the storm becoming worse by the minute. We peered through the windscreen at the faint outline of the road lit by the headlights and eventually, the flashing blue lights of the police cars glowed ominously through the rain. There were two police cruisers and an ambulance. Jen pulled up at the side of the road and we climbed out. 'Can you bring my bag Harry?' she asked. I nodded and strained to haul the big black bag out of the back of the Hilux; Fury jumped down and followed us. The thunder and lightning were quite regular now and the rain heavy and relentless. Jen walked over to one of the officers, the other was helping the paramedics load a very large woman into the ambulance. 'I've come from The Sanctuary about a black bear,' she said.

'Yeah, right, thanks for coming out. The Halifax city vet is out on call so we had no choice but to ring you. Think it's going to have been a wasted journey though. Sure it must be dead,' said the officer.

'Where is it?' asked Jen.

'Over there in the road,' said the officer, pointing at a black mound near the centre of the Highway. There were cones around the whole area and orange safety lights flashed to warn passing traffic. Fury was already over by the mound and above the sound of the rain and thunder; I could hear him growling, head low and hackles up.

I hauled out Jen's medical bag and followed her past the wreck of the brown Ford estate that was side on to the road, its front badly smashed and vivid skid marks clearly visible against the slick wet tarmac. Glass fragments glistened and crunched underfoot. The black mound looked like a heap of old clothes and it was only as we got much closer that it was possible to tell that it was an animal.

81

Jen pulled a torch out of her pocket and shone it downwards. I stifled a gasp as the black mound suddenly became a large, fur covered body. The bear was curled into a ball and there was a stream of blood mixing with the rain and trickling along the tarmac. Jen knelt beside the body, which looked about twice the size of Fury and felt around for a pulse. 'It's alive,' she said, 'just.'

Fury had stopped growling now, but his head was still low and his muzzle only centimetres from the bear. I suddenly realised that Fury was not taking the least notice of the thunder. Most dogs would be jumpy and scared; not Fury, he took no notice of it at all. 'What do we do?' I asked.

We've got to get it into the back of the truck and back to The Sanctuary. There's nothing I can do here. It's almost certainly got severe internal injuries. Get the tarp out of the truck Harry.'

I raced back to the truck and with dad's help pulled a large green tarpaulin out of the back of the Hilux. When we got it back to Jen, she asked us to spread it on the ground next to the bear.

'Now, we've got to roll it on so we can drag it' said Jen. All three of us crouched and pushed with all our might. Slowly, the bear turned over and flopped onto its other side, on top of the tarpaulin now. I realised that the bears head was close to mine now and then it opened its eye and I found myself looking into the yellow eye of a mighty black bear. It just looked at me though, too weak to move, breath coming in shallow rasps. But I could tell it was regarding me with an intelligent gaze before, slowly, the eye closed.

Jen ran back to the Hilux to back it up to us whilst dad and I began hauling the tarpaulin. It was hard work and the great bundle moved just a few inches with each heave. With the Hilux just behind us now, Jen slid out a ramp and clambered into the back of the truck. The weight of the bear was too much and I could feel myself tiring quickly. Unexpectedly, Fury pushed between me and dad and grabbed a mouthful of the tarp in his jaws. He pulled back with rapid jerks of his head and straining legs. The tarpaulin moved and kept moving. Within moments the bear was at the bottom of the ramp. Jen tied the tarp to a metal tow rope and used a handset to begin the winch inside the back of the truck. The tarp took the strain and began to slide up the ramp, the black bear lying motionless. As soon as the bear was in the back of the Hilux, we quickly climbed in and pulled away. The orange warning lights and flashing police lights quickly faded into the distance behind us.

Chapter 11
A Strange Christmas Day

It was a long night. Once we got back to The Sanctuary we got a gurney and after a lot of effort, manhandled the bear onto it. Dad helped wheel it into the operating theatre which was attached to the back of the house. He said we needed to go home but I begged to stay and help Jen operate. Finally he gave in and a call to mum organised his lift. Once he was gone I washed and went to find Jen. She was in the little room where the old x-ray machine was housed. Jen was holding up the new x-ray to the light and staring at it intently. 'It's in a bad way,' she said, 'Broken pelvis, broken hind leg and a fracture to the skull. To say nothing of the internal bleeding we're going to find. It might be kinder to put it to sleep.'

'No, please!' I cried. 'You can save it, I know you can.'

'Maybe I can save it,' said Jen looking at me seriously, 'but the question is should I? It's in great pain and there'll be a lot more even if the operation is a success. It would be kinder to put it out of its misery and suffering right now.'

'It looked at me,' I pleaded. 'Out there on the highway, it looked at me and I knew it wanted to live.

'It'll take all night. Are you willing to stay and help me?' she asked.

'Yes,' I said. 'I'll stay.'

Sometimes, over the next few days I wished I hadn't pleaded so hard for Jen to save the black bear. Not now of course, but back then; I just couldn't have imagined how difficult it would be. Fury was anxiously pacing backwards and forwards in the kitchen.

We scrubbed up and I had to put on 'theatre blues' - sterile trousers and top which were too big for me - a mask and gloves. The bear was already prepared, lying on the operating table with tubes running into its body. There was also a tube in its mouth and a heart monitor machine beeped a constant rhythm in the background. I was trembling and sweating as Jen prepared to make the first cut. I was convinced I was going to faint and make a complete fool of myself. Jen made the first incision on the bear's side close to where the broken pelvis was. I closed my eyes without thinking. 'Suction Harry!' said Jen insistently.

Opening my eyes, I froze at the site of the wound and the blood. 'For God's sake, Harry, focus. I need suction now!' she said sharply.

Jerked to my senses, I thrust the air suction pipe into the wound to remove the blood that was welling up. From that point on the thought of fainting didn't cross my mind. I was totally engrossed in the wonders that Jen performed. She found and stopped the internal bleeding in different places then went about pinning the damaged pelvis. She had to carefully bend titanium brackets to the exact shape needed before drilling holes into the bone and screwing them into place.

Occasionally I would glance over at the theatre door, only to see Fury's face as he rested his front paws on the sill and stared in, watching the progress of the operation. It must have been terribly tiring for him and he kept disappearing only to return a few minutes later. Finally, Jen set the broken hind leg and ensured there was no pressure on the brain from the fracture. It took six hours altogether and by the time the bear had carefully been put into a cage for recovery it was nearly five in the morning. Wearily, we changed and Jen went to bed. I said I would stay on the sofa. I was asleep almost before my head hit the cushion.

A rasping on my face woke me from the deepest sleep. As I struggled to force my protesting eyes open, Fury's tongue caught me a smacker right on the mouth. I spluttered and sat up, wiping my mouth in disgust, 'Oi, get off. I was having a lovely dream.'

Fury trotted over to the door to the veterinary surgery and pawed at it. 'What is it boy?' I asked, getting up and walking over. I went in and immediately saw the black bear, lying in his cage, eyes open, looking at me. He hadn't moved but as I walked over, the intelligent eyes kept following me. As I got to the cage I reached out - I knew I shouldn't, this was a dangerous wild animal after all - and scratched the bear under the chin. He kept regarding me with those dark eyes, his breathing shallow and fast. I began stroking him along his belly and gradually his eyelids drooped and his breathing became deeper and slower. When I was sure the bear was asleep, I quietly left with Fury following close on my heels.

Jen appeared at just after eight. After checking the bear and telling me things looked good so far, we both set about mucking out and feeding the current crop of guests at The Sanctuary. Even on Christmas Day, the same routines needed following, the animals had their needs and no one else would do the work.

At nine, we were ready for breakfast, toast, butter and jam, honey or peanut butter. Gabe joined us, looking rough but saying he felt a little better. 'You best get home,' said Jen as we finished washing up. Your family will be missing you and it is Christmas Day after all.

I nodded. 'Can I come back later to see how the bear's getting on?' I asked.

'Yes, of course you can,' said Jen. 'You did a great job last night. I wouldn't have managed it without you.'

I blushed at the praise, secretly pleased with the words. 'Gabe will drive you back to the lighthouse,' said Jen.

Christmas Day at Peggy's Cove was different from back in Britain. Far fewer presents to start with, but I didn't mind that. We had a family agreement that us children wouldn't spend more than five dollars on each person and mum and dad no more than fifty dollars on each of us. We all looked at our little gifts with smiles on our faces, happy and knowing we didn't need the piles of presents we had been used to in previous years. My present from mum and dad was great; a dome tent, second hand, but that just meant it was better quality with a little bit of dirt on it. With all the wilderness in Nova Scotia, I knew I would make frequent use of it in the year ahead.

Christmas dinner was really special. We had booked a table at the Sou' Wester; it was expensive but mum said it was a special treat and it would be almost impossible to cook a proper full roast dinner on the little stove in the lighthouse.

Sandy Banks greeted us at the door with a glass of bubbly for mum and dad and fruit juice cocktails for Sal and I. It turned out to be all locals; Ma was there with her daughter's family and six or seven other family groups from the fishing families of Peggy's Cove. Molly wasn't there though, or the families of the two older boys who had picked on me.

It started with each group on its own table, but by half way through, everyone had joined in to one big group. At the end of the meal, the tables were pushed back and there was singing; dancing and even some really lame games; that even though they were so truly awful, turned out to be hilarious. All through the celebration, Fury sat across the road next to the same shed I had seen him near when I thought I was being hunted by some supernatural beast. The party held no interest for him, but he wanted to be as close to me as he could.

By eight the party was winding down and my thoughts began to turn to the bear once more. I asked dad if I could go over to The Sanctuary. He said yes, but he couldn't drive me as he had been drinking. I didn't mind, the fresh air would do me good.

As soon as I appeared at the door, Fury trotted over and followed just behind me as I began the walk to Cranberry Cove. It was cold and dark and I was glad to see the lights of The Sanctuary ahead. Gabe and Jen had had a quiet day, not least because Gabe was still recovering from his stomach bug and Jen was exhausted from the exertions of the previous night. I helped feed the patients their evening meals then went in to the Recovery Room to see the black bear. He was being kept sedated so that he didn't try to move around and further damage the pelvis and hind leg that needed to heal. As I knelt beside the cage with Fury at my elbow I saw that the bear's eyes were open again, slightly glazed but fixed on me. I began stroking his big belly again and he seemed to move slightly to make it easier for me to reach. Eventually he went back to sleep as the sedation overcame him. I stayed for a few hours and sat with the Munroes. 'He's about eighteen months to two years old I would guess,' said Gabe. They often stay with their mother till about that age, and I would have expected him to be hibernating at the moment. It's a bit strange all round to be honest.'

'Is he all right now?' I asked. 'Will he make it?'

'It's very early days yet. It will take a couple of weeks to be sure if the breaks and fracture are healing properly and the next twenty four fours are vital as that's when there's the highest risk of infection from the wounds setting in.

Well, after hearing that I wasn't about to go home was I? I checked with the Munroes, made a call home and was ready to spend the rest of Christmas Day and all of Boxing Day keeping a vigil over the bear. I had to think of a name for him. Gabe and Jen wouldn't approve as it was a wild animal and naming them just got you attached, but I knew he needed a name.

I made a little bed up next to the bear's cage in the Recovery Room using some old cushions and a couple of blankets Jen lent me. It was warm in there all the time so the animals would be comfortable. Fury lay beside me, nose on my lap, peering at the black bear intently; he never once growled.

It was a long night. I tried to stay awake, stroking the bear's coarse fur but kept drifting off. At about two in the morning, as I woke again, I realised the bear was tossing its head from side to side. I reached in and felt its nose; it was red hot; I didn't need Jen here to tell me that an infection had taken hold. Before she went to bed she had told me that the bear had had full doses of antibiotics and there was nothing more she could do at present, so I was on my own. I knew that there was a good chance that after all that surgery and surviving the crash and operation, the bear could still die because of this infection.

In the surgery was a refrigerator for drugs and a freezer as well where some types of food were kept. I took a dishcloth from the kitchen and filled it with ice. Quickly I wrapped the cloth around the ice and placed it on the back of the bear's thick neck. I held it there with one hand whilst with the other I stroked and scratched its stomach. The bear continued to toss its head and rock its great body from side to side, each breath a rasping, torturous strain. I was sure he was about to die and there was nothing more I could do.

But he didn't die. At around six, the rocking of his body stopped, followed gradually by the shaking of his head and the ragged breathing slowed and became more relaxed.

The crisis had passed and I knew that he was going to make it, I was as sure as that.

The effort of looking after the bear had completely exhausted me and shortly after the crisis I fell fast asleep, one arm still stretched out over his front paw and belly.

A slight pressure on my hand woke me and the first thing that met my eyes was that of the huge mouth of a black bear wrapped around my hand. I could see the fangs glistening white encasing it. I was too afraid to pull my arm back in case the movement caused him to bite down, it might take my whole hand off. I felt like sobbing in fear until I realised that the bears eyes were looking at me and then I realised that Fury was still beside me, head on my lap. I looked down and he was wide awake, just looking at the bear, no growling, no sign of concern at all. I looked back at the bear and it opened its mouth, freeing my hand. Slowly, cautiously I drew it back with a profound feeling that I had never been in any danger at all.

'Your name is Banka,' I whispered. The name had just popped up from the depths of my memory. 'Banka Mundi is a Hindu god of hunting... well... to be perfectly honest it's a goddess, I learnt about her at school, but the name fits you.'

I reached in and stroked the bear's muzzle; he in turn nodded his head under the pressure of my hand, as if saying, 'Yes, my name is Banka Mundi.'

Chapter 12
A New School

Over the next few days, Banka the bear showed signs of recovering. He started to eat and though he could barely move, he was trying to haul himself around the cage on his good front legs. By New Year's Eve he was hobbling around the cage. Jen said a human would have been in bed in hospital for six to eight weeks with the sort of injuries the bear had suffered, but of course a bear is a wild animal and has no idea what has happened to it. Banka was still in a great deal of pain and had taken a swipe at Gabe a few times when he got close to the cage. 'He's a wild black bear and bloody dangerous,' said Gabe showing me a long scratch along his forearm where Banka had raked him with his claw.

I didn't say anything. I hadn't told anyone I had named the bear; I knew they wouldn't approve.

Molly didn't appear at The Sanctuary in all the time Banka the bear was there, which was odd. I asked the Munroes about it but they just looked uncomfortable and said she sometimes stayed away for days at a time.

On New Year's Eve we had a family meal at the lighthouse. We played some games and saw the New Year in with a glass of sparkling wine each and a toast from dad for the next twelve months to be as happy and successful as the first few weeks we had spent in Canada. We all raised our glasses and drank to that.

On New Year's Day I couldn't help the mounting concern I was feeling for Molly. She still hadn't turned up at The Sanctuary and I had seen lights on in her house, so they hadn't gone away. I plucked up my courage and at about ten, walked in to Peggy's Cove with Fury behind me, keeping watch.

Molly's house stood by itself and looked in a pretty sorry state. The pale blue paint was flaking away and the wooden shutters at the windows had missing slats. Apprehensively, I climbed the porch steps. Fury wouldn't climb them; he sat resolutely at the bottom and refused to budge, no matter what I said. I knocked at the door and after an awful long time, it opened a crack. I saw part of Molly's face peering at me from the gloomy interior. 'Hello,' she said.

'Hello yourself,' I replied. 'You haven't been around all over Christmas and I was getting a bit worried.'

'There's no need to worry,' she said in a flat voice. 'I've not been very well that's all. I'll be right as rain for school on Wednesday.'

The thought of starting school had not entered my mind for weeks and to hear it now, and that it would start in just two days was a bit of a blow. But there was something else in Molly's voice; something sad; something scared. Something wasn't right. I pushed the door open against her protesting hands. 'What's wrong Mo...' I faltered as I saw Molly in the light. There was a nasty black and yellow bruise around her right eye and also the brown smudges of fading bruises showing just below the sleeves of her t-shirt on either arm.

'I fell in the kitchen.' Molly said, eyes looking at the floor and arms hugging her thin body.

I could feel a white anger rising in my chest and I could hear Fury growling behind me. I couldn't speak.

'Oow is 'at?' a deep slurry voice called from back in the darkness of the house. I saw a shambling figure at the end of the hallway; Fury's growling had turned to proper snarling and I realised he had crept up the steps and was now at my feet, body close to the ground and his hackles up.

'I've got to go,' said Molly fearfully. 'I'll see you at school Harry.' She swung the door shut in my face.

'What did you make of that?' I asked Fury. He just looked up at me with those big brown eyes. I knew what was going on with Molly now and it made me at once incredibly sad for her and unbelievably angry with the monster she was forced to live with. I made a vow to myself there and then that I would help her escape if it was the last thing I did.

Two days later, I was standing in front of mum and dad at seven fifteen in the morning. It was to be my first day at school. Dad could take me in to Halifax with him on his way to work but I didn't think it would do my street cred any favours turning up with him every morning; so I had opted to take the bus both ways from the start. Sal stood beside me in leggings, a short skirt and a thick jumper. There was no school uniform and I was wearing jeans, a sweatshirt and trainers. I was a bit nervous... well, who wouldn't be? Fairview Junior High School was on the outskirts of Halifax on the west side. Junior was Grades 7 to 9 or ages 12 to 14 years. Sal was in Grade 9 and would move on to Senior High School the following year.

'You scared?' asked Sal with a malicious smile on her face.

'Only that they might realise you're my sister,' I said.

Sal punched me hard in the arm. 'You want to be nice to me,' she said, 'just in case some of those Halifax kids decide they don't like you. I'm popular; just you remember that.'

'Knock it off you two,' said dad. 'Sal I expect you to look out for your brother.'

'No way dad!' I said passionately. 'I can look after myself. Sal can stay with her goofy friends and keep as far away from me as possible.'

'I'll make sure he's all right,' said Sal, flicking me round the head.

'Right, off you go,' said mum shooing us out of the door.

By seven thirty we were standing at the bus stop. Fury had come with me of course, but as we had approached the bus stop, he had become agitated and clearly didn't like the group of people waiting for the bus. When we stopped and stood with the others, Fury seemed to make a decision; he walked off, looking back frequently until he was lost around the corner of the street. I was surprised and a little hurt that Fury had left me like that; I had actually been worried about how I was going to leave him when it came time to board the school bus. I didn't have to worry about that as he had decided to desert me.

The two older boys who Sal told me were in her Grade sneered at me as we walked up then ignored both of us completely. Molly was there too, but apart from a slight nod in my direction, she kept her back to me. I was disappointed by her attitude, but realised that she probably had a lot to deal with in her head. I probably needed to let her have some space. Sal chatted to me about Fairview Junior High. She was happy the two boys were ignoring us; she clearly didn't like them either.

We were only at the bus stop for a couple of minutes before the big, yellow school bus rumbled up. As we clambered aboard, Molly took a seat near the front, head against the window and staring out at the bleak winter landscape. I sat next to Sal near the middle. There were already ten or twelve children on the bus, mostly fifteen or sixteen year olds who went to Halifax West High School. As the bus drove out of Peggy's Cove and reached the junction with Highway 333, Sal said, 'would you look at that; Fury didn't just leave you, he came to see you off... look,'

I looked out of the window and sure enough, there was Fury, sitting next to the bench I had sat on when I first chatted to Molly all that time ago. I smiled to myself.

The fifty minute trip took us along many side roads to pick up small groups of students here and there. By the time we were five miles from Halifax, the bus was nearly full. The journey passed quickly and before I knew it we had pulled up outside Fairview Junior High.

Now, I'm not going to bore you with all the details of that first day; let's just say it went pretty well. The Canadian school system is pretty cool and I felt more independent and as if I was being treated as a young adult right from the start.

Junior high schools are fairly small, about five hundred kids so I didn't feel too lost and already felt like I knew the place by the end of the day. It was quite cliquey, but nothing unusual there. I had the novelty value of a British accent and a story of sorts to tell. I had a crowd around me at every break and the start of each lesson, firing questions at me. It was quite cool actually. The only blip to spoil the day was when the two fourteen year old goons from Peggy's Cove cornered me in the dining hall. I was just putting my plate and cutlery away in the cleaning racks when the tray was knocked out of my hands; and there they were, right in my face. One of them put his arm around my shoulder, but there was no friendliness in his voice. 'Settled in real quickly ain't ya limey?' the taller one said.

I didn't reply. The other kid - he had spots and greasy, swept back brown hair - jabbed me in the chest with his finger. 'We don't like you limey. We ain't happy you come to Peggy's Cove. Why don't you just run off back where you came from?'

'Look, I didn't want to come here, it was my parent's decision. I haven't got anything against you. Can't we just be friends?' I asked.

That didn't go down well. The taller boy shoved me and I fell back against the stacked trays which crashed to the floor. There was a sudden silence in the dining hall and a group of kids who had been in my classes that morning made their way quickly over to me. 'Friends?' the tall one grunted, 'oh no, I don't think so. You better watch your back dog boy, cause we're goin' to be lookin' for you.' They walked off; glaring at the group of Grade 7 students I had talked to during the morning. They were quite protective and told me the two louts were in Grade 9; well known troublemakers and bullies. A small consolation was that they would be moving on to Senior High School the following year. Not very comforting as they lived in Peggy's Cove, so I would always see them around and they would still continue to use the same school bus.

At the end of the day, two boys in my home form, Chaz and Tony stayed with me till the bus arrived at the front of the school. 'We're just gonna make sure them slime balls don't hassle you,' said Chaz. I knew right then that these two were potential friends.

The ride home was uneventful. The two morons, whose names I had discovered were Brad Williams and Kent Moon sat at the back and tormented some of the other kids around them. I sat next to Sal near the front. Molly was on her own again, huddled into her seat, face turned to the window.

At home, mum bustled around me asking lots of annoying questions and becoming frustrated at my monosyllabic answers. The conversation went something like this:

Mum: Did you have a good day?
Me: Yeah.
Mum: What did you get up to?

Me: Not much.

Mum: Was the bus ride okay?

Me: Yeah.

Mum: Did you make any friends?

Me: Some.

Mum: Do you think you'll like it there Harry?

Me: Dunno.

I know it was a bit rude, but what did she expect, I was nearly a teenager after all. You don't really talk to your parents about that sort of thing do you? Dad realised that and when he got home later, all he asked was, 'Did it go all right son?' and my answer of, 'Yeah, fine,' was enough for him.

The rest of the first week at Fairview Junior High was just as good. I settled in quickly and Chaz and Tony started to become real friends. In fact, it turned out that they were on the school soccer team and I needed no encouragement to go along to a training session after school. Back in Britain, I was just an average player, but here I was a bit of a star that first session and the coach took me aside and said he wanted to put me into the school soccer squad. I was overjoyed.

I found the lessons quite challenging, mainly because the curriculum was completely different to the one in Britain, but I knew if I worked hard I would be okay. Every day I left, Fury would walk with me to the bus stop and then race to the bench at the junction with the highway and there he would be waiting for me when I got back. He must have stayed there all day every day, waiting for me to return and as the bus passed he would get up and lope back so that he was waiting for me when I climbed off. No one else went near him as the growl that started deep in his throat was enough of a warning for all to stay clear. Before I knew it, that first week was over and it was the weekend.

I was tired on Friday evening and went to bed early with Fury curled up beside me. I was awoken by a knock at the door; it was only six thirty in the morning by my watch. I opened the door and there was Molly, wrapped up against the chill of the morning. 'You coming to The Sanctuary?' she asked, keeping her eyes down to the ground.

'Yes,' I said. 'Just give me a minute to get dressed. You want to come in and wait?'

'No, I'm good just here thanks,' she replied in her small voice.

Chapter 13
Goodbye Banka

Five minutes later we were walking down the peninsula with Fury trotting along behind. 'Do you want to talk?' I asked, not looking at her.

'It's difficult,' she said quietly.

'Look, Molly, you shouldn't have to put up with being treated like that. It's abuse. Your father should be in prison. Why does your mother let it happen?' I said angrily.

'He's not my father,' Molly snapped hotly. 'Not my real father anyhow. He's my stepdad; his name's Mason Brook. My real father was a fisherman. He died when his trawler went down off the Grand Banks in a storm seven years ago, when I was five. Mum met this guy in a bar two years later and he'd moved in inside a month. He was drinking even then, but mum ignored it; she just wanted a man back in her life; someone to look after her. But he never did that. He couldn't hold down a job; didn't want to. He sponged off my mum; who worked all hours as a cook at The Sou' Wester.

Then she took ill, all of a sudden and the doctor said it was cancer. He gave her a month to live and she got real ill real quick. I looked after her; he rarely raised more'n a finger. And then she was gone, just like that. The cancer grew so quickly there was nothin' the doctors could do. She just wasted away to nothing. It was like she just evaporated, sort of. Anyway, he organised the funeral and that's when I found out that I would have to live with him. Mum had written a will and though everything went to me, she had made him my legal guardian and he had control of the little bit of money she left and of the house until I'm eighteen. There's nothing I can do until then.'

'But he can't treat you the way he does; it's abuse. The police would put him away for years,' I said, horrified.

'They probably would,' said Molly, 'but what would happen to me? I'd be taken into care, put into an orphanage most likely and the house would be sold. That house is all I got left of my mum and dad and I don't want to lose it. Not at no price. Do you understand that Harry?' There were tears in her eyes now and I felt the stinging hotness in my own. I blinked rapidly to try and keep the tears at bay.

'Yes, I understand,' I said. 'But I will think of a way to help you,' I promised. 'Just you wait and see.'

Molly just smiled at me and sniffed.

This was going to be a big day at The Sanctuary. It was the day that Banka the bear was to be released back into the wild. Molly and the Munroes had all helped in his recuperation from his injuries, but I was the only one that he allowed to touch him without growling or snapping with his great jaws. I was always careful, after all he was a five hundred pound wild animal that could have torn me limb from limb, but I knew he wouldn't hurt me. He seemed to know that I had helped him and he would even take chunks of fresh meat from my hand.

As we neared The Sanctuary, I felt a great sadness that I would never see him again after the release. It had to happen of course; he would never survive in a zoo after living free and black bears are certainly not pets. As we walked into the yard at the back of the house, I saw that the Hilux was already loaded. Banka was in the cage in the back and he turned baleful eyes on me as I approached. I reached in and stroked the fur on his back; he wouldn't have allowed anyone else to do that. 'You ready boy?' I asked in a whisper. The scar from the operation was well healed now but the fur had only just started to grow back where he had been shaved. He was restless in the strange new surroundings of the truck and swayed back and forth, peering at the yard around him. Gabe came out of the house, 'You ready Harry?' he called.

I nodded and climbed into the front seat. Once Gabe was at the wheel we set off. It was just the two of us as we had decided the day before. The Hilux bounced over the rutted track up to the freeway and we were soon cruising along Highway 333. The road was nearly empty we passed Yankee Bay, where Banka had been hit by the car. Gabe turned off the highway onto a small track and drove along it until we were in the hills, half a mile back from the coast. The great pine trees towered over us and the smell of pine resin was strong in the air. 'This is it,' said Gabe. 'Can't get much further without getting stuck and it's near enough to his own territory for him to find his way back to wherever he came from.'

'Can I say goodbye?' I asked quietly.

'Best not Harry. You know he's a wild animal. Just let him go.' There was a hollow feeling in the pit of my stomach at the thought that this would surely be the last time I saw Banka the bear. Gabe reached down and flicked a switch, with a creak and gentle whir, the back of the crate rose up on electric pulleys. I looked at Banka, eyeing the grill suspiciously through the small back window of the cab. It took a couple of minutes before he plucked up the courage to stick his head through the opening and a couple more before he eventually flopped gracelessly onto the ground. Banka didn't just leave though. Slowly, the black bear plodded round to the front of the truck and stood there for a moment looking at us sitting inside; I could almost have convinced myself he was looking at me alone. He opened his mouth and gave a long mournful wail before turning his great body and galloping ponderously up the slope before disappearing into the trees. 'He was looking at you; did you see?' said Gabe. 'I've never seen that before; darned if I have.' Gabe turned the ignition and swung the truck round. I looked out of the rear window as long as I could, but Banka did not reappear; he was gone.

Chapter 14
Camping Trip

The next few weeks drifted past with not much happening. School was fine and I played a couple of games for the soccer team, helping to win both and scoring twice. I was a bit of a hero actually and the Coach was overjoyed.

The last weekend in January, the school had arranged a camping trip for us kids. They're hardy sorts those Canadians. You'd never have got schools in Britain camping in January and it was much colder in Nova Scotia. Out of the 500 children in the school, 98 were going. Chaz and Tony, who had become my good friends, cajoled me into going, assuring me we would all share a tent. Mum and dad agreed and on a cold, windy and wet Friday morning I waited at the bus stop with my new rucksack, bulging with warm clothes and a sleeping bag strapped to the top. It was much earlier than normal as a different bus to the usual school bus was picking most kids up directly from school then collecting the few who lived in the sticks on its way to the campsite. The place we were going to stay was called The King Neptune Campsite. The name had rung a vague bell until I realised it was at Yankee Cove, where Banka the bear had been hit by the car.

As I stood waiting for the bus, my heart sank at the sight of two slouching figures, each carrying their own huge rucksack coming towards me. They were unmistakably Brad Williams and Kent Moon. They stopped about twenty metres away and glared in my direction. Fury, standing by my side let out a low growl and watched them intently. The bus came about ten minutes later and I hugged Fury before clambering aboard. I put my rucksack in the overhead rack and sat down towards the back. I watched Fury trot over to the bench I knew he liked to sit beside whilst I was at school, but he had only got halfway before I saw Kent Moon swing his arm just before getting on the bus. Fury let out a yelp and I realised he had thrown a stone at him. Fury turned and groggily stumbled back towards the bus, teeth bared in a snarl of anger. Kent Moon had already jumped into the bus though and the doors were hissing closed. I stood and tried to get out of my seat and rush to the front, 'Why did you do that?' I cried.

'Do what Limey?' Kent Moon called back, 'looks like your flea ridden mutt ain't feeling too good. Maybe you should stay behind and look after it.'

There was nothing I could do and they knew it. 'Come on, sit back down,' said Chaz from the seat opposite. 'They're jus' a couple of idiot losers.' I took my seat again, face flushed with anger. I watched Fury out of the window as the bus pulled away. He looked shaky on his legs and I thought I could see blood on the side of his huge head as he stared back at me. I prayed he was alright and felt pure, white anger course through my veins at those two bullies. They would pay for hurting Fury.

We arrived at the campsite by eight as it wasn't far at all. We were quickly checked off by the teachers and soon Chaz, Tony and I were inside our Indian style wigwam tent unpacking our clothes. It was quite cosy with thick furs on the floor and surprisingly spacious. The tents had been allocated by year groups so all the surrounding wigwams had children I knew quite well in them. The two creeps from Peggy's Cove were on the far side of the camp thankfully; I really didn't know what I would do after what they had done to Fury. I would only get into trouble I was sure.

I didn't have time to think about revenge however, as the activities we were to do began straight after we had unpacked and followed on one after the other; fire-lighting, trail finding, making clean water, identifying different fungi - all before lunch.

We sat around the camp fire for lunch. 'You worried about your dog?' Chaz asked.

'Yes,' I said. 'He might have been badly hurt; he might need treatment.'

'I'm sure he'll be alright,' said Tony. 'He was trotting after the bus when I looked out the back window of the bus.'

'Are you sure?' I asked. 'He was alright then was he?'

'He looked okay to me. Don't worry about him Harry; it'd take more than a stone to hurt Fury.'

I felt relief flood through me. After that I began to enjoy the camping trip a whole lot more.

By the time we had exhausted ourselves with a whole afternoon of challenging but fun bush-craft tasks we were famished. The whole camp of ninety eight children plus teachers and the instructors were seated around the enormous camp fire, which soared four or five metres into the air, sending glowing sparks high into the night sky. By eight O'clock we had all had our fill of hog roast and baked potato and were singing campfire songs (I didn't know any of them, but joined in enthusiastically).

At nine, the instructors told us we were going out into the woods to play 'capture the lantern'. There was general screaming and whooping as all the kids got to their feet and rushed after the instructors. After ten minutes or so we were in complete darkness apart from the torches of the eight instructors guiding us. Suddenly, all the torches were turned off and we were left in utter darkness. There was silence all around. A bright light flickered on far off in the distance. 'See that light there? The lead instructor's voice sounded eerie in the darkness, 'That's the lantern you got to get to. It's about two hundred metres away. You gotta get there any way you can. But here's the catch; us instructors are going to be searching for you. If we hear you and shine our torches on you, you're out and you gotta return here and start all over. So, quiet and sneaky does it.' The lead instructor's torch snapped on and the beam waved over to the left. 'The thick forest begins over there a ways; that's the boundary that side. Don't go no further that way.' The torch beam swung over to the right. 'And that way there's a stream about a hundred metres off or so. Don't go beyond that. Now if you're all ready, spread out. Us searchers'll get in position and you start on my whistle.'

There was electric excitement in the air; it was a real spooky atmosphere out in the wild, utter dark but with all those people around you. Tony grabbed my arm and with Chaz close behind we charged out to the left. A minute later a shrill whistle blast signalled the start of the game. It became dead quiet again as everyone slowed down to a crawl so they wouldn't be heard. Apart from the gleaming lantern in the distance, there was complete darkness; it was only just possible to make out vague shapes a few metres away. Every now and again a torch would suddenly stab a bright beam around and shrieks of despair told us some kids had been spotted and sent back to the start.

We kept close to the ground, moving from one tree stump or fallen log to another in short spurts. After we had covered about half the distance to the lantern I trod on a twig which snapped like a bullet going off. A torch beam flashed on and swung round looking for me. Before I could move I was caught in the white light, 'Gotcha!' called a girl's voice. 'Back you go,'

I silently cursed my clumsiness and turned. I felt a hand on my leg and saw Tony's face looking up at me; neither he nor Chaz had been spotted. "We'll come back with you,' he whispered.

'No,' I said. 'You're doing well. Keep going; I'll try the other side and see if I have more luck. See you at the lantern.' Tony patted my leg and I made my way back to the start point. There was a steady stream of kids returning and setting off again as the torch beams stabbed on and caught the creeping attackers like startled rabbits.

I jogged off, to the right hand side this time, hands held out to stop myself colliding with rocks, trees or anything else. After a few minutes I reached the bank of the stream which marked the edge of the playing area. There didn't seem to be anyone this far over as far as I could hear, so I edged along the meandering bank of the stream, thinking I would try and get past the lantern and attack from behind.

I sneaked one step at a time, listening to the whoops and screams of others as they got close and were caught. I was almost level with the lantern when I stopped suddenly. I had the feeling there was someone close by, an instructor or another kid creeping up to the Lantern? There was a definite noise behind me and I turned to see what it was. My head was snapped to the side as something smashed into my face. I fell to the ground, stunned and dizzy. I tried to get to my feet. I was hit again, across my back; I sprawled among the damp moss and must have lost consciousness for a while.

My eyes fluttered open but I could see nothing. I was being dragged by the arms by two people. My mind was confused; what was happening? 'Back with us Limey?' a harsh voice asked. I recognised it as once... Kent Moon.

'What are you doing you psycho?' I stammered through a mouth that only just seemed to work. I couldn't think straight and my mind was foggy and confused.

'Just taking you for a little walk,' said the voice of Brad Williams. Get you nice and lost.'

I've no idea how long they dragged me; it seemed like hours, but was probably only twenty minutes or so. The cries and screams of the kids playing Capture the Lantern had completely disappeared now and we were in thick woodland. Eventually, my two kidnappers let go of my arms and I flopped to the ground. I tried to get up straight away, but one of the boys kicked me hard in the stomach. 'Where you goin'?' Kent Moon hissed. I fell to the hard ground again, wheezing for breath. 'We'll see you again soon... Prob'ly,' continued Moon. I couldn't answer as I was still winded.

'I told you we'd get you in the end,' Brad Williams said.

'Why?' I gasped, 'What have I done to you? I barely even know you.'

'You ain't done nuthin', we just don't like you Limey. Guess we just like picking on you. Seein' ya squirm,' said Kent Moon in a sarcastic, wheedling voice. And that's when I knew that I could have been anyone, it didn't matter where I came from, who I was, I was just the new boy on the block and that made me their target. My situation suddenly looked considerably worse. Here I was, out in the wilderness, no-one knew where I was and I had no idea which direction help might be in. I pushed myself backwards slowly with my hands and feet until my back came up against the trunk of a giant spruce tree.

'Where ya goin' there buddy?' said Brad Williams, the menace all too clear in his voice. A torch flicked on and I was dazzled as the beam was pointed straight into my face. As I shielded my eyes from the dazzling light with one hand, one of my tormentors kicked me

115

across the face, hard. My head snapped sideways and flashing lights danced before my eyes. My head rang and the pain of the blow exploded behind my eyes. I could hear them both moving round in front of me. I covered my head with my hands to try and protect myself from the next blows that I knew would fall. They could do what they wanted to me out here and no-one would know. The panic began to rise through me at the realisation of how much danger I was really in. It was then that the growling began. It was over to the left of where I lay and the torch beam, joined by a second flicked in that direction.

'What was that?' said Kent Moon, his voice edgy and scared.

'Bear?' said Williams. 'Somethin' there anyhow.' The beams of their torches flicked from side to side across the bushes and trees that surrounded us. The growling continued, rising in intensity. My attackers retreated a few paces until they were standing right in front of me, facing towards the intimidating roar.

'I know what it is,' I said slowly. 'And you might just want to walk away now before it's too late.'

'You just shut up Limey!' shouted Moon. Unexpectedly, he turned and lashed out at me with his boot. The undergrowth about ten metres away erupted instantly as something flew from within it.

Williams turned his torch and the beam illuminated two flashing disks, like mini suns and a beast in mid leap, jaws wide and lips drawn back revealing fearsomely sharp teeth. Williams screamed as Fury hit him with the full weight of his body. He was knocked flying with one arm held between Fury's jaws. Fury shook him like a rag doll and he screamed like a baby. Moon, who had stood, terrified to the spot now kicked out at the dog. Fury loosed his grip on Williams and turned on his new attacker. The dog lunged and grabbed Moon's leg. Instantly he was thrown off balance and screamed in pain. 'Help me!' he screamed. That was when I realised that Williams was holding a knife in his hand. It flashed in the light of one of the torches that had been dropped on the ground.

'Fury!' I shrieked. It was too late though. Williams jumped at him and I saw the knife rise and fall twice. Fury let go of Moon and jumped away.

The stricken Moon struggled to his feet and began to run off, his injured leg dragging behind. 'Come on, let's get out of here!' he cried.

Williams looked like he was about to move towards Fury, but the dog barked viciously, flecks of saliva flying from his mouth as he also advanced; crouched low. Williams thought better of taking Fury on face to face and he turned and ran after Moon.

Fury sank to the ground, panting. I crawled over and hugged him tightly. I couldn't believe he was there, but I had known the instant I heard the growl that it was his. He must have followed the bus somehow... after Moon and Williams had thrown the stone at him. Had he thought I was in danger? I didn't know, but, here he was and he had saved me. I held my friend close, until I realised that he hadn't licked me or made much of a move at all since lying down; then I felt a sticky wetness on my hands. Looking round frantically, I saw one of the torches Moon and Williams had carried lying close by. I reached for it and shone it on my hand... It was covered in blood and as I turned the beam onto Fury, I saw that his fur was wet with his own blood too.

Chapter 15
Alone

With Moon and Williams gone and Fury lying quietly beside me, I felt utterly alone again. I couldn't see anything in the impenetrable blackness of the woods at night except the small area the torch lit . The few stars that were visible were largely blocked out by the huge trees around me. I had begun to shiver. Even though I was wrapped up in four layers, I had been doing nothing for some time. I knew my body was losing heat rapidly and I was completely lost. But my main concern was for Fury; he lay beside me breathing shallowly, but his life could be ebbing away with every passing minute. There was a lot of blood

I laid on the ground for a few more moments thinking what to do, the back of my head, where I had been hit by the log or branch still throbbed terribly. The vapour from my breath billowed over me like a cloud of smoke. It was getting colder and a frost was already starting to form on the bark of the tree nearest me.

I had to slow the bleeding from Fury's wounds. Quickly I took off my parka and gloves, I undid my belt and pulled off my outer shirt. I tore it into rough strips and wound them round Fury's body. There were two stab

119

wounds in his side close together. Once the makeshift bandages were wrapped round, I used my belt to tie and keep them in place. It seemed to work, but I knew I had to get Fury out and to a vet as quickly as possible. I dressed again and found two strong sticks. I hadn't yet warmed up from having removed my shirt, but knew I would have to sacrifice my parka as well. I stuck a stick through each sleeve and tied the ends to make a 'v'. This way I had a stretcher of sorts that I could drag Fury on. Carefully I laid my dog on the stretcher and lifted the tied end. I would have to keep moving so that my body produced heat. I only had a vest and thin undershirt on now and the cold was a killer. Hauling the stretcher behind me, I stumbled off, not knowing where I was headed, the stretcher bounced over the hard ground and Fury let out an occasional whimper, each one like a knife to my own heart.

Everything was so still and quiet with only the occasional hoot of an owl to break the silence. As I trudged along I was shivering almost uncontrollably. A mist had risen up and the trees had thinned as the ground rose upwards. Eventually I realised I could go on no further; I wasn't going to find help out here and I had no idea if anyone was even searching for me. If the camp instructors had done a roll call at the end of the Capture the Lantern Game, they would have noticed I wasn't there and started searching immediately; but had they?

Or had the whole group just gone back to camp? Chaz and Tony would have raised the alarm as soon as they realised I wasn't there but had they got back to camp yet? How much time had passed since Williams and Moon had ambushed me? It was unlikely those two would own up to having had anything to do with my disappearance. For the moment I was alone and I had to try and keep us both alive till morning; it would be easier for them to find us in daylight.

I couldn't feel my fingers or toes anymore. I needed shelter. Somewhere I could try to get warm and keep Fury warm; but where?

I pulled one of the torches I had rescued out of my pocket and flashed the beam around me. Close by, the ground rose sharply in a low cliff and as I shone the beam of light across the rocks, a dark patch caught my attention. I hauled the stretcher behind me, but it was like a lead weight now and my back was screaming in pain at the stooped position I had to adopt to pull Fury behind me. The ground was bare and covered in loose stones now so my feet continually slipped as I tried to haul myself up. It took ten minutes and my knees and hands were grazed and scratched. Eventually, I reached it and sighed with relief; it was a cave and it might give me the shelter I needed to survive. I turned and dragged the stretcher a few metres into the cave mouth which was so low I had to stoop to get in but quite wide.

Once Fury was inside, I slumped to the floor, breathing heavily and shaking so badly I couldn't even have taken my gloves off if I'd wanted to. I checked Fury and for an awful second thought he was gone, but his eyes slowly opened and he gazed at me mournfully, unable to even raise his head now. The blood had dried hard on his fur and I couldn't find any sign of fresh blood, so the bandages seemed to be working.

It was then that I realised there was a strange smell in the cave. It was strong and smelt like mouldy fur and animal droppings. My half-frozen brain took long seconds to realise that this was the smell of bear. I had smelt it often in Banka's presence. Panic rose in me immediately. How stupid I was; a cave in the wilds of Canada? Of course it might be the home of a bear, and as if to confirm my fears, there was a terrible, guttural howl from the depths of the cave.

Instantly, I was on my feet. I hauled Fury's stretcher round and began yanking it downhill as fast as I could. There was another roar from the cave but it sounded closer. As I stumbled over the stony ground I became aware that I could see more of what was around me. There was a lightness to the sky and some of the clouds were streaked with silver and red. Dawn was coming. I had been wandering, lost, all night.

Another enraged roar split the air from behind me. This one did not seem to echo as much as the last and glancing over my shoulder I saw a great black bear standing at the cave mouth, swinging its great head back and forth in annoyance. Suddenly, it saw me and lumbered in pursuit, its great paws sending stones flying in all directions.

'Oh God, this is it Fury,' I croaked. I turned and ran anyway; there was no way I could outrun a black bear, especially pulling Fury behind me but I offered up a silent prayer for help. The ground seemed to disappear some ten metres ahead of me and my surprise soon turned to despair as the reason why became clear. I had reached the edge of a cliff. It ran off in both directions as far as the eye could see in the early morning half-light. Peering over, I saw that it was a good thirty metres down to the rocks below. No way could I get down on my own, let alone with Fury; and I couldn't leave him.

The bear roared once more and this time he was only ten metres away. I stood in front of Fury, lying on the makeshift stretcher with my back to the dizzying drop. I waved my arms and yelled at the top of my voice. The bear reared up on its hind legs, fangs exposed and dripping. It wasn't scared of me in the slightest.

The beast stood, swaying for a few moments, its beady eyes fixed on me. And then I saw something, a dark shape moving down the slope near the cave, behind the bear. It was moving fast and as it approached I saw it was another black bear. What difference did it make I thought to myself, this was the end whether it was one bear or two that I faced.

The roar that the new bear made as it closed on me had a startling effect on the one rearing in front of me. It turned its head, looking for the source of the sound and the new bear, far from charging at me and tearing me to pieces, hit the rearing bear hard from behind. Both bears tumbled to the ground, but the newcomer had the advantage and was above the other. It bit at it and raked it with its giant paws. The bear that had chased me tried to fight back for a few seconds before giving up. It pulled itself away and ran for it, loping off along the top of the cliff.

I stood, amazed, gazing after the fleeing bear until the heavy, snorting of the victor drew my attention back to the new threat in front of me. The bear just stood there, looking at me. Frowning, I looked harder in the quickly lightening morning and was able to make out more and more detail. 'Banka?' I said, hesitantly, and then again, louder, 'Banka!' I stumbled forward and threw my arms around Banka the bear. He had heard my prayer and had come to save me. I could feel the tears streaming down my face as I nuzzled the great beast's fur and he in return rubbed himself against me and sniffed at my hair. 'Thank you

Banka,' I whispered. 'You saved me, but now I've got to save Fury.' I let go of the bear and went over to check on my dog. Banka the bear plodded over and nuzzled at Fury's face.

At that moment, a thunderous crack shattered the air and Banka took flight before I could do anything about it. The rifle shot was followed by shouts as a group of people appeared at the opposite end of the cliff to where the first bear had fled. It was a rescue party, at last.

Five minutes later, I was wrapped up in a blanket and drinking hot, sweet tea from a thermos one of the men had brought. The rescue party had been following my trail for hours and had fired a warning shot when they had seen Banka apparently attacking me. They were incredulous when I told them I knew the bear and it had saved my life.

My only concern then was for Fury and it was a relief when I heard a helicopter was on its way to take me to hospital for a check-up and that it would take Fury as well.

Less than half an hour after I had been about to be killed by a wild black bear, I was seated safely in a helicopter with Fury beside me, unresponsive, but breathing. Things might be alright I thought as the ground fell away and the roaring helicopter carried me to safety.

Part Two

Stella

Chapter 16
A New Arrival

The next few days were a complete blur. The helicopter had stopped off at The Sanctuary at Cranberry Cove and there, Gabe and Jen rushed him into surgery, after first checking I was alright. I wanted to stay but the medic on the helicopter wouldn't hear of it. I was whisked straight to the hospital in Halifax where mum and dad joined me later. Mum was all tears, hugging me and kissing my face whilst dad just clapped me on the shoulder, but I could see his lower lip trembling as he tried not to cry as well. It was all really embarrassing to be honest, but I knew they couldn't help it; they were so relieved that I was okay. Even Sal, who trailed in behind them had said, 'Glad you're okay,' after punching me in the arm.

The only thing I could think about was Fury. Jen Munroe called and left a message with the nurse that he was stable but in a serious condition. They had operated and stopped the internal bleeding and he just needed time now she had said. I felt a wave of relief flood over me as I heard that. I knew he would be alright then and my thoughts turned to the two lunatics who had caused me and my dog to go through all this.

The Royal Canadian Mounted Police arrived shortly after and that's when things got interesting. I told them the whole story, from when Williams and Moon had grabbed me during the game of Capture the Lantern to when the rescue party turned up. They didn't say much about Banka the bear saving me, though I caught them smirking at each other when I said it and realised they didn't believe a word. But, would they believe my story about Williams and Moon? They seemed to and said they would be going straight round to interview them.

I was made to stay in hospital over-night, just to make sure I was okay.

The following morning, the doctors told me I was fine, that I had been very lucky not to suffer any frostbite and that the bump on my head had caused a slight concussion but nothing more. Dad drove me home and I made him drive straight to Cranberry Cove. As soon as the car stopped, I jumped out and ran round to the Recovery Room where animals who needed more intensive care or who were recovering from operations were housed. Jen Munroe was in the yard, cleaning the yard with a hose, 'Well, look who it is,' she said, laying the hosepipe down and embracing me in a huge hug.

'Is he alright?' I asked. 'Is Fury okay?'

'Go take a look for yourself,' she said.

I raced in and there, in one of the cages was Fury. The moment he saw me he began to whine and tried to struggle to his feet. 'Stay down boy,' I soothed, sticking my arm through the bars and stroking him. Fury lay back down and raised a leg, feebly, to encourage me to stroke his belly. 'It's good to see you,' I said softly. There was a drip leading into his paw and his side was shaved where Gabe and Jen had operated. Fury was clearly weak and looked quite sorry for himself, but there was no doubt that he was on the mend. I stayed with him for half an hour before Gabe appeared. He was dressed in overalls and a thick parka.

'Good to see you Harry,' Gabe said, shaking my hand enthusiastically. 'It was a close run thing with old Fury there. Lost a lot of blood and there was internal bleeding as well, but your work staunching the worst of the bleeding gave him a chance and that was all he needed. Fury is one tough old hound. He was determined to pull through. Two, three more days and he'll be good as new.'

'Thank you,' I said.

'Don't mention it,' said Gabe. 'But there is something you could do to help if you like.'

"What?' I asked, eager to get involved.

'There's an otter on its way in. A ranger found it caught in an illegal trap over by Prospect Bay. He's bringing it in now. It'll need Jen and me to operate. I could do with your help with lights, instruments and so on. Molly's going to be lending a hand as well. You up for it?' Gabe asked.

'You bet,' I said. I was thrilled that Molly would be there as well. She hadn't been allowed to go on the camping trip as her step-father had refused to pay.

I had wanted to help out more in the theatre since I assisted in the operation on Banka the bear. But of course I was too young; only qualified veterinary nurses should have helped in theatre, but as Jen said, 'We're a charity. No money to hire anyone else, so if an operation needs both of us, it's ask one of our volunteers to step in or let the creature die. And I'm here to save lives. I know what decision I'm gonna make.'

It was Sunday morning, so no school to worry about. Dad wasn't happy; he thought I should be at home resting, but he gave in in the end. Gabe and Jen were scrubbing up by the time I got back and I did the same. At that moment, Molly walked in. She smiled shyly at me as she began to wash, 'Hello there, I hear you tried to escape from the camp-over and got lost in the wilds,' she said innocently.

'Huh!' I huffed. 'It was those jerks Williams and Moon. They attacked me and left me in the middle of nowhere. Fury took them on and made them run off, but not before they stabbed him. I thought we were both going to die.'

Molly looked stunned, 'Williams and Moon? I saw a police car outside one of their houses on my way here. I hope they get put in prison for what they did to you and Fury.' She looked puzzled for a moment, 'How did Fury get to be there? You couldn't have taken him to the camp-over.'

I shook my head, 'I just don't know. I guess he followed the bus. He could have been worried about me after Kent Moon hit him with that stone. But it would make him one smart dog to have managed to follow a bus and then keep hidden until he had to make a move to save me. But I can't think of any other explanation.'

'Well, I think he is special. You're lucky he chose you,' Molly said. 'And you're lucky you got found before any wild animals picked up your trail.'

'Lucky!' I said, incredulous. 'I had to keep moving all night to stop from freezing to death, I was worried stupid about Fury and then to cap it all, I nearly got eaten by a bear.'

Molly giggled, 'A bear? Come on, if you'd been attacked by a bear, you wouldn't be here now; it would have made mincemeat of you.'

'It nearly did,' I said indignantly. 'Until Banka turned up and saved me. He attacked the other bear and it ran off.'

'You're kidding,' said Molly.

'Are you serious?' said Gabe, and I became aware that he and Jen had been listening to our conversation.

'I'm serious,' I said. 'But I'm pretty sure the police didn't believe me.'

'How do you know it was Banka?' asked Jen.

'I'd know him anywhere,' I said. 'But if you mean proof, I could feel the scars from where you operated on him when I hugged him.'

'You hugged him?' asked Gabe amazed. 'Well I guess it must have been Banka then. I'm just stunned any bear would act like that. You seem to have some strange effect on animals Harry.'

I smiled shyly at that and carried on scrubbing up.

Before long we were all in theatre gowns and waiting for the patient in the consulting room. We heard a car screech to a halt and a burly ranger in brown state uniform and a Stetson hat rushed through the door. Grasped in his hands was an old cardboard box and as he put it down on the examination table, we all peered in. 'Not even sure it's alive,' the ranger said scratching the back of his head.

'How'd you find it?' asked Gabe, gently lifting the otter out of the box. It was a beautiful thing; long and sleek with fur that seemed to shimmer under the lights.

'Pure chance,' the ranger said. 'I was out checking fencing round the reserve at Prospect Bay when I seen this poor critter caught in a snare. Must have been there at least a day, too weak to struggle no more and the wire had dug in good and proper round its neck. Just cut it loose, damning those inhuman poachers and called you on the radio.'

Laying the poor creature on the table, it was possible to see the soft fur around its neck was matted with dried blood and there was bare flesh visible where the wire had cut in deeply. Jen felt all over the otter's body. Its stomach seemed to be swollen and I thought this might be a sign of some serious internal injury.

'It's pregnant,' said Jen. Molly and I looked at each other in amazement. 'It's pretty near full term as well,' Jen added. 'Let's get her into theatre and see what we can do.'

Gabe carried the otter into the theatre where we all put our masks on. It took Jen and Gabe a couple of minutes to examine the otter fully. Eventually, Jen said, 'There's nothing we can do for her. She's lost too much blood.'

'But what about the babies?' gasped Molly.

'There's still movement there but without the mother they stand no chance,' said Jen.

'But if they're still alive they could be hand reared couldn't they?' asked Molly desperately.

I saw Gabe and Jen look at each other. 'It's possible they could, but they would probably die in a few days,' said Gabe. 'And hand-rearing them would mean they would never be able to be returned to the wild. What sort of life could they lead?'

'I'd look after them.' Molly pleaded. 'I'll do whatever's needed, really I will.'

Gabe and Jen looked at each other again for what seemed like an age before Gabe gave an almost imperceptible nod of the head.

'Alright, we'll try to save the babies,' said Jen. 'But it'll take a heck of a lot of work on your part.

'Molly nodded her head wildly, 'I'll look after them, no matter what it takes.'

'The mother's gone,' said Jen quietly. 'Right we've got to get a move on if we're to stand any chance of saving the pups.' The next twenty minutes were tense as Jen performed a caesarean section to remove the otter pups from their mother. Molly and I passed instrument after instrument and swabbed away blood when needed. Jen pulled the first pup free and I was amazed that it was no bigger than two of my fingers. It looked lifeless and Gabe rubbed it vigorously to get the blood pumping whilst Jen concentrated on the next pup. The second otter pup looked just as lifeless as the first when Jen pulled it free and my heart sank. We were too late.

'This one's gone,' said Gabe in a tired voice. The poor pathetic looking thing lay on the stark green cloth covering the operating table.

'There's no sign of life here either,' said Jen who had just stopped massaging the second pup. It was even smaller than the first.

'That's it,' said Jen, 'just the two pups. I'm sorry Molly.' She gently laid the limp body by its mother.

'Please don't give up!' cried Molly. 'Let me try.' Before Jen or Gabe could stop her, Molly had picked up the smaller pup and cradled it in the blanket Jen had been using. She rubbed the little things stomach with her thumbs through the thick towelling. She was sniffing back tears and I felt unbelievably sad, both for the tiny little creature in her hands and at the thought of her own unhappy life. Gabe raised his hand to stop Molly from continuing with the pointless task when suddenly there was a tiny sneeze and then a mewling as the little otter pup suddenly sprang to life, its heart began to beat and it breathed in its first lungful of air in the world.

We all cried out in amazement as the little otter, not much bigger than a matchbox, lying on its back in the palm of Molly's hand, waved its tiny front paws to the world as if saying hello to us all.

'It's a female,' said Jen quietly.

'She's called Stella,' said Molly in a voice full of emotion. And that was how Stella joined our little band, and what a difference she was to make.

Chapter 17
Oil

It was touch and go for the next three weeks as to whether Stella would survive. She was so small, with eyes that wouldn't open for a fortnight and totally reliant on her mother... who wasn't there. Well, 'a' mother was, but it wasn't her real mother and it wasn't even an otter. Molly took on the role and lived at The Sanctuary for the first three weeks, taking the first week off school, claiming she was sick.

Stella needed feeding every few hours and the only way to feed her with her real mother gone was with an eye-dropper. Stella drank the milky mixture the Munroes made up as if she was starving (and she probably was). Molly would sit by her cage, a towel on her lap, the tiny otter lying in the centre whilst Molly dripped the food into her mouth. Apart from drinking the milk, Stella remained blind and asleep all the time in those first few weeks; but she began to grow and at the end of a fortnight, she had doubled in size.

Molly had started school again at the beginning of the second week and went to The Sanctuary every morning and evening. Gabe told me she slept on the floor beside Stella's cage most nights and that when he had phoned her step-dad to check if this was alright, had got the distinct impression he couldn't care less where she stayed.

I went and helped out as normal and once again had Fury to keep me company. He had come home after four days and although he walked very gingerly and limped around with his head down most of the time, he was well on the road to a full recovery and barely left my side every moment I was around Peggy's Cove.

Brad Williams and Kent Moon were nowhere to be seen since I had returned from hospital and I was sure glad about that. I hoped the police had arrested them. The Royal Canadian Mounted Police called at the lighthouse one evening and dad, mum, Sal and I sat at the table whilst they filled us in with what had happened. It turned out that Moon and Williams had come up with some story about having been lost themselves during the Capture the Lantern game at the camp-over, claiming they had never laid eyes on me. The police knew they were lying as both boys had quite serious animal bites which though they said they had been caused by some mongrel dog they had tried to pet, the police had thought otherwise. The officer told us he was sure they came from some big dog and matched where I had described Fury had attacked them. The boys had maintained their innocence and the police had no real evidence apart from my word against theirs.

Those two thugs were going to get away with it. Dad was outraged and bellowed at the police officers, but there was nothing they could do. They did add that there had been uproar in the local community though, after people heard what the boys were supposed to have done to me and Fury. Most people believed the story I had told you see. Williams and Moon had such bad reps already that everyone just knew they were guilty. The officer said there had been threats against the boys and their parents as well (who apparently were no-good troublemakers themselves and far from strangers to the law). And a week earlier, both families had just upped and left one night. They had packed up and moved away. Clothes, furniture and what was most important, their sons.

I was angry that they had got away with what they had done to me, but at least they were gone and I could live in peace. The officer said they would be keeping tabs on the boys to ensure they didn't think about coming back and causing more trouble.

With all the unpleasantness of Williams and Moon behind me, I could relax and enjoy school, my new friends and help Molly with Stella.

At three weeks old, I was there whilst Molly was feeding the tiny otter pup, with a small baby's bottle now, when the tiny eyes flickered and strained and before long, opened. Stella took her first looked at us with her dark brown eyes. We looked at her, amazed by how beautiful she was; cuter even than a puppy dog.

The next few months flew by. School was great; I was star of the soccer team and top scorer. I regularly saw Chaz and Tony a couple of times a week after school and got the late bus back to Peggy's Cove. Fury was fighting fit again and his old grumpy self around other people. Mum and dad had decorated the upper floors of the lighthouse and bought some new furniture now dad's job was secure.

Stella just grew and grew. With Molly feeding her from a baby's bottle through the night and Jen taking over during the day, at two months old, she was too big to stay in the runs in Shed 1 where the marine mammals were housed. Gabe came up with an ingenious idea; at the side of the main house at The Sanctuary there was an old, disused larder, once used for storing food and keeping it cool before fridges were invented. The old door leading into the main house had been bricked up and the glass in the single, tiny window was smashed. Gabe turned up one morning in the middle of March with the back of the spare jeep filled with old caravan windows. 'I got them from the breakers yard over the other side of Halifax,' he told us. 'Help me get them out.'

By the time Molly and I had finished, there was a pile of ten or so aluminium framed windows lying on the ground. Gabe wouldn't tell us what he was going to do. So we got on with our chores. It took him a week to finish and he had gone to extraordinary lengths to keep it secret from us. He had erected a sort of fence with bamboo canes and old sheets. Whenever Molly and I were at The Sanctuary he would shoo us away if we got too close.

In the meantime, Stella was becoming a real handful. She was frustrated by the small space of the run and began gnawing at the metal mesh. She would hurl herself around the run and even tried to burrow through the concrete floor.

On Friday evening, as Molly and I were feeding the few guests that were recuperating at The Sanctuary, Gabe called us over. Jen joined us as we made up the audience. Gabe made a little speech; 'I have laboured day and night for the last week...'

'And left all the work you were supposed to do for me!' butted in Jen pointedly.

Gabe continued, after a stern look at his wife, 'I have laboured long and hard... in order to complete this wondrous piece of architecture. Built for the benefit of our new acquaintance,' here, Gabe paused and indicated the slender shape of Stella, wriggling furiously in Molly's grasp in a desperate attempt to get free. She held her firmly, wrapped in a thick cotton towel.

Stella's head peered around constantly, her inquisitiveness insatiable. Everything interested her. Gabe continued, 'A new home for our rapidly growing friend,' He suddenly grabbed a rope and yanked. The sheets that had hidden his secret project fluttered to the ground and the three of us were left staring open-mouthed. Stella, also, had ceased her non-stop head turning. She was looking fixedly at what lay behind the sheets.

It was a marvel really... A shoddily built marvel, but a marvel all the same. The old larder now had a wire mesh door and inside, the small space had been made into a living area with ramps and shelves as well as a sleeping box. The really amazing part, however, was the construction outside the front of the larder; it was about four metres long and two high by about a metre deep; wooden framed and covered with the old caravan windows. About eighty percent of the front and ends was glass and it was filled with water. An aquarium was what it was, or at least a playground for an otter. We all clapped and whooped loudly as Gabe took several bows.

The next step was to introduce Stella to her new home. She didn't need any encouragement; the moment Molly let go of her, she leapt to the ground and in the graceful, lopping hops she had developed, disappeared inside the larder door. After a few moments of scratching and banging as she raced around

141

her new home, Stella's head appeared at the entrance to the water tank, which was the old window to the larder with the glass removed. She stood there for a moment, whiskers twitching, staring at us then at the water below. We stood with bated breath; Stella had not seen water so far in her short life except in the small amounts she drank. With no more hesitation, Stella threw herself forward and she pierced the water like an arrow. The beautiful, sleek body shot around the tank, disappearing at one window, only to reappear at the next. It was as if she had been swimming for years. She would occasionally stop at a window and look at us with happy, glinting eyes. Thus did Stella get her new home and there was soon a sign on the door which read 'The Water Park'.

Not everything was great at Peggy's Cove and in the surrounding coastal area of Nova Scotia; the Canadian government had granted oil drilling rights to a giant multi-national company and the first rig was already on its way. Apparently it would be about fifteen miles out to sea in a line between Peggy's Cove and Cranberry Cove. Gabe and Jen were beside themselves and wouldn't even talk to Molly and I about it. As a last resort I went to talk to Ma at the store. As usual she was bustling about and the smell of cinnamon rolls filled the air. 'Sit yerself down,' she called as I entered. 'Try one of my cinnamon buns.' I did as instructed, perching myself on a stool at the counter; Fury lay at my feet.

'Ma, I need to understand why Gabe and Jen are so worked up about this new oil field opening up off the coast. They won't talk to me about it.'

'Reckon everyone's wound up about it round these parts. For starters, fishing's a big employer here. Most families have links to the sea through men folk working the fishing boats and everyone knows that oil and fish don't mix, not lest you're frying it to eat that is. And secondly, this here's a haven for wildlife. Pulls in tens of thousands of visitors and that's money spent in local businesses like mine. You get an oil spill, it ain't so pretty anymore and people stop coming. That's when peoples' livelihoods dry up. It may be fine an' dandy for the great big company that's taking the oil and getting all that money for it, but it don't spell nothing but worry and hardship for us as live here if anything goes wrong.'

'So that's why the Munroe's are so annoyed?' I asked.

'It's a lot closer to home for them. They was involved in the clean-up after the Exxon Valdez disaster in Prince William Sound over in Alaska. Real nasty business. Tens of thousands of sea birds, seals, otters and others covered in oil. They saved some, but not nearly enough and everything covered in that putrid, evil smelling, poisonous crap. And that's not to mention the millions of fish that died and rotted. It fair makes me want to cry, and I weren't even there. They was and they helped, but it took its toll. They know what can happen if there's an oil spill and they don't want to see it happen here.' Ma was quiet for a moment. 'There's a big meeting and protest rally in Halifax on Saturday if you and your family want to come along with me.' I said I would and was sure mum and dad would as well. I left Ma's feeling very low. I had grown to love this place in the short time I had been here. The beauty; the wilderness; the wildlife; and of course, the people. It was very special to me and I didn't want to see it ruined.

Chapter 18
The Kraken

I was surprised at how angry mum and dad were about the opening of the oil field off of the Nova Scotia coastline. Dad ranted about how any serious oil spillage could wreck the local fishing industry and how his own job could be put in jeopardy if the fish stocks were seriously depleted (who would want new trawlers then after all?).

In the end, we all went to Halifax with Ma in her big station wagon, along with most of the population of Peggy's Cove in a convoy of old cars. It was the first Saturday of April and the rally started at noon in a big park close to the centre of Halifax. When we arrived there were already thousands of people milling around and we took our place on a grassy bank with a good view of the platform where the speakers would talk to us from.

I won't go into detail about the protest; there were brightly coloured banners calling for the oil company to stop its plans and others stating the environmental damage that could befall local communities. There was singing and everyone was in great spirits. It was the first speaker that I really remember. A Professor named Dawson, Peter Dawson and from his first word he had the whole crowd, which must have numbered more than ten thousand, in the palm of his hand. He started with an outline of the beauty and diversity of the wildlife of the area before moving on to the possible effects of pollution caused by this new oil field. I could see how angry the Canadians were and they cheered when Professor Dawson urged the government to reconsider and the oil company to look to less ecologically fragile locations. I cheered along with everyone else as he finished.

There were more speakers and by the end I felt that the Canadian government must change their minds, so many people were against the idea, how could they not? After the last speaker, the crowd began to break up. We all went for a burger at a local restaurant and I was surprised that Ma seemed quite down. 'It'll change nothing,' she said tiredly. 'Too much money involved. The government will give some reassurances but the oil company will still come and then we better just keep our fingers crossed, that's all.'

By the time we got home it was already dark. Two days later, whilst watching the news, there was a report that said that despite public concern, the government had given the go ahead for drilling to begin off the southern coast of Nova Scotia. I was stunned, but mum and dad didn't seem surprised at all. I felt stupid at having thought that what all those people at the protest wanted might actually have been listened to.

The following Thursday, Molly called round really early and dragged me off to The Sanctuary. It was still only 5.30 in the morning and the dawn light was just the merest smudge on the horizon. Fury padded on ahead, ears pricked up for the slightest sound. There were always a few fishermen around, getting ready for an early start. We waved at them and carried on. When we reached Cranberry Cove, Jen and Gabe Munroe were standing on the beach. We joined them and the four of us, with Fury sat, leaning his heavy body against my leg, were silent for a while, staring out across the vast Atlantic Ocean. 'Thought you might want to see the unwanted visitor arrive,' Gabe said, the anger barely concealed in his words.

It was another ten minutes before a ship appeared around the peninsula that hemmed in Cranberry Cove. It was a big ship, about a mile off shore, squat and powerful looking. It wasn't the ship that made my jaw drop but the thing it was pulling behind. From behind the headland, about two hundred metres astern of the ship, something else was appearing. Great towers of steel rose high into the sky like the legs of a gigantic insect. Gradually, an enormous structure that the towers were attached to began to show itself. The whole thing dwarfed the ship that pulled it. It was dark and ominous looking with steel protrusions sprouting in every direction. It was for all the world like a monster from hell. My mind was filled with visions of the terrible Kraken; the awful sea monster from Greek mythology and I was sure that this is what it must have looked like to those terrified ancient Greeks, three thousand years before.

A terrible feeling of foreboding filled all four of us as the ship moved on out to sea with the great drilling platform towed behind. By that evening, it had been placed on the sea bed about fifteen miles out, but still visible on the horizon; and given the name Orion V.

Although the drilling had started, it would take weeks before the oil rig drilled deep enough to reach crude oil. Life went on and spring was in full bloom by May. Stella, having grown into a young adult full of mischief, had soon escaped from her new home. After a few days of panic over where she was and if she was alright, it became apparent that Stella was going nowhere. She often disappeared at night, only to be found safe and sound, swimming in her glass fronted pool the next morning. Stella would run round the yard with Fury snapping at her heels in playful leaps. He would lick, nuzzle and chew gently on her head as if she was a fragile toy, but he never hurt her once.

Molly spent as much time as she could with Stella at The Sanctuary. It seemed to take her mind off her life at home. I knew she was having a real hard time with her step-father as she became more distant and once I saw bruises on her wrists. She pulled her sleeves down to cover them up when she realised I had noticed them and I didn't ask; I knew how they had come to be there. I think it was Stella that kept Molly going if I'm honest; she was chatty and friendly with me but Stella gave her unconditional love and never asked her questions. She liked that.

We were all having a great time as spring drew on and summer approached. There didn't seem to be any problems from the new oil platform and most days Fury and I would go on long walks along the coast, me with an old pair of binoculars dad had found for me and Fury with a piece of driftwood in his mouth, tossing it in the air one minute and chewing it to splinters the next. I would watch the birds and try and spot whales or seals out at sea.

The weather kept improving and it was comfortable hiking in just a shirt by the end of May. It was one Sunday afternoon I think when I sat on a boulder, the gentle Atlantic swell lapping at the pebbled shore and Fury sniffing up and down the high tide line when things changed. I was scanning the ocean for the tell-tale spurts from the blowholes of whales when my binoculars came to rest on the ugly shape of the Orion V oil platform. Up until now there had been no sign of life from this distance, but as I watched, a bright flame blossomed at the top of the highest steel tower. It died back slightly but stayed burning like a signal fire, with dark, black smoke curling into the sky above. I sat back, resting my binoculars on my knees. The Orion V had struck oil. And now the black gold had been found there would be no stopping them. More oil rigs and the huge oil tankers to transport the oil would be here in the blink of an eye. I looked left and right and smiled at the beauty of the landscape and the incredible range of living things that called it home; I prayed silently to myself that it would remain so.

Chapter 18
Storm Warning

It was about the beginning of June when we noticed some strangers around town. They arrived in a couple of trucks and parked in the Sou' Wester car park. There were about six of them, all big and tough looking; they wore work clothes and hi-viz jackets. The men had equipment with them and spent the next two days using instruments to take measurements; how far things were, how high and so on, just like surveyors do before something gets built. They wouldn't say what they were up to and rumours started pretty quickly.

As suddenly as they had arrived, they disappeared. Some people thought they worked for the oil company, most people felt uneasy and suspicious and everyone had their own theory about what would happen next.

Despite all the ideas the townsfolk had come up with, what did happen was still a shock. Letters arrived at several properties in Peggy's Cove. They were letters from the solicitors department of the oil company stating their intention to compulsorily purchase the properties. We didn't get a letter, but we did get a visit; a man from The National Trust of Canada arrived, very apologetic, explaining that as the owners and landlords of the Peggy's

Cove lighthouse, they had received a letter and not us. It seemed that the oil company wanted the lighthouse as well, or at least the land it stood on. He was very angry; saying the lighthouse was a part of Canada's heritage and that the government were obviously in on it. We just stood there. It didn't belong to us after all and we had only lived there for six months or so... but it was home and it felt like we had been there all our lives. The thought of having to move was a real shock.

There was a town meeting the next evening and every resident of Peggy's Cove, all one hundred and thirty seven people were squashed in to The Sou' Wester restaurant as there was no village hall. There were representatives of the local planning office and from the oil company there, sitting at a table at the front.

Sandy Banks, the owner of the restaurant led the meeting and it was very bad tempered. The townspeople were angry and the planning officers said little apart from apologising that their hands were tied and the government had given the go ahead. The representative from the oil company was roundly booed as he stood up to speak. 'I'm truly sorry,' he began. 'Our company is not out to ruin your community or to destroy your town, but we need depots on shore and some maintenance facilities. In fact, we estimate that our company will be bringing no fewer than seven hundred and fifty jobs to

Nova Scotia and that's a mighty lot of opportunities for local people and a lot of money to spend in your businesses.' There was a lot of shouting after that. Local people didn't want throwing out of their homes and the business owners didn't care about more money coming in if it came at the expense of losing friends and the small community feel they had grown up with.

When the meeting broke up, things hadn't gone well. The oil company were determined to push ahead with their plans and it was obvious they were prepared to walk all over anyone who tried to get in their way.

The following week we got an official letter telling us to vacate the lighthouse in a month's time. Mum was really upset as she had made some good friends in Peggy's Cove and dad said he had never felt like he had belonged anywhere as much as he did there. I felt just the same.

The next Saturday morning, after Molly and I had finished our chores at The Sanctuary, we took a walk up the cove with Stella prancing around and Fury nipping at her tail. 'My step-father's over the moon we're being forced out,' she said. 'The oil company are paying twenty percent above market value and he'll get to move us to Halifax where he's always wanted to be.'

'How do you feel about it?' I asked.

Molly looked at me and I realised she was close to tears. 'I was born in that house and my ma brought me up there and died there. It's the only connection I got to her and now it's being taken away from me. Oh, and as it's being compulsorily purchased my step-father gets the money and has to look after it in my name. How long do you think that'll last? He'll have drunk every penny away inside a year.'

We walked on for a while; Stella and Fury were totally oblivious to the terrible future we both saw for ourselves, wrenched away from this beautiful place to who knew where and probably never to see again any of the people I had grown to love. I glanced at Molly who was kicking pebbles into the sea and knew she was one of those I loved; not like that obviously, but like a sister or something. Anyway, I knew I would really miss her, just like Jen, Gabe, Ma, Sandy Banks and yes, Banka the bear and Stella. All might just be memories in a few short weeks. My darkest thought however was whether Fury would come with me. He had stayed out in the wilderness after his last master left him; mightn't he do the same with me when I left? Might he decide to stay here in the place he had known all his life? I felt the tears welling in my own eyes as Molly turned to face me, her own small face streaked and wet. 'Come on,' she said, 'let's get back home.'

The removal van was booked and a new place for us to live in downtown Halifax had been arranged by The National Trust of Canada. I had just got home from school; at least that wouldn't change when we moved, and I had the radio on; I rarely watched TV any more. The local news report was on and the announcer was talking about the weather. A storm was approaching. It sounded like a big one, there had been a few since we had arrived but this sounded much worse. It was coming out of the North Atlantic and there were shipping warnings for a dozen areas of the ocean.

By the time we all sat down for dinner at seven, the reports of the approaching storm were worse. It was due to hit us at around midnight. 'Lucky we live in a lighthouse,' dad said.

Mum looked thoughtful, 'You're right. It might even be pretty spectacular to watch from the light room.'

Sal and I looked at each other eagerly; this was an opportunity not to be missed. It was Friday night and the prospect of a front row seat at the top of a lighthouse to watch the storm of the century was too good to be true. Sal asked mum if we could go to the store and get popcorn. Five minutes later we were wrapped up and on our way. The wind had picked up considerably and Fury kept barking and running off as if he was chasing something only he could see before returning, sheepishly, only to charge off once more.   Purple grey, angry looking clouds were tearing across the darkening evening sky.

Ma's stayed open late at the weekends but even so there were a lot of people around Peggy's Cove for eight on a Friday night. As I took more notice, I realised the locals were preparing for the imminent arrival of the storm. They were busy fixing wooden shutters across their windows, stowing outdoor items and tying down bigger objects like benches and swings on porches. It was quite scary actually, like being in a war and waiting for the enemy to attack.

We hurried and got our supply of sweets with Ma waving us out the door and yelling for us to get back home safe and sound as quick as possible.

The walk back was tough; the wind was frighteningly strong and the thunder clouds boiled overhead. As we reached the peninsula the first clap of thunder rolled over us, making the hairs stand up on the backs of my hands. The storm was still miles off yet but we realised we should be indoors looking out by now.

By the time we stumbled up the steps to the lighthouse, our arms ached from carrying the shopping bags and Fury's ears were flat against his head as thunder claps split the air and lightning flashed in the distance. It was nine O'clock.

By ten, we were all sitting in the glass light room perched at the top of the lighthouse. The light above us shone its fierce beam of white light out over the dark Atlantic in slow sweeps. Mum and dad sat on pillows to one side whilst Sal and I had two thick duvets pulled round us. No one could have as good a view of the storm that night as we were going to experience. Sal passed me the popcorn whilst she sucked Dr Pepper noisily through a straw. I could hear Fury howling down below; there was no way he could climb the ladder to this floor. The sea looked like it was set on a hob with the heat on full, bubbling and hissing; the white flecks of foam livid on each wave as it crashed against the shore. 'They're eighteen to twenty feet high now!' dad shouted above the roaring howl of the wind outside.

'Do you see the light over there?' mum shouted. Looking out, I could just make out the flicker of a flame, far off and lost behind sheets of rain or huge waves one minute before flickering into sight again the next.

'That's the Orion V rig off Cranberry Cove,' I said. 'I didn't even know you could see it from here.'

'I wouldn't want to be on it tonight,' said Sal. 'Not in this weather, all that way out at sea.'

The rain slashed at the glass and made it impossible to see anything at all for a few seconds. When the squall cleared for a moment and we could once more see the enormous waves crashing against the shore and writhing across the sea as the light moved across it, there was a flash. The horizon lit up for a moment before fading away, but not entirely. Where the faint flame had been only moments before there was now a boiling fireball, raging into the air like a roman candle going off.

'Oh my God!' dad whispered, his voice only just audible above the storm. 'That was the Orion V. Something's gone badly wrong out there.'

Chapter 19
Inferno

Dad wanted to find out what was going on, so, leaving mum and Sal with a pair of binoculars and the radio on full blast, waiting for news reports, he dragged me downstairs to get some bad weather clothing on before making our way out to the car.

The storm was in full swing and outside of the protection of the robustly built lighthouse, I felt small and afraid. Fury wouldn't be left behind so I let him into the back of the car. Dad drove recklessly down the rough peninsula track and by the time we screeched to a halt in front of The Sou' Wester there was already a sizeable crowd assembled. The Orion V rig was hidden from view here by the headland, but the glow from the fire that had erupted was visible over the hillside. 'What's going on Sandy?' dad shouted, his voice almost lost in the driving wind.

'Reckon that rigs gone up,' Sandy replied.

'But how could that happen?' dad asked desperately.

'Dunno, maybe the lightning, or a pipe ruptured in this weather, and then a spark. Don't know. But it'll be lucky if there's any survivors.'

'How many men are there on the Orion V?' dad asked, holding his head in his hands.

'Not sure, eighty five... a hundred... a lot anyways.'

'We've got to do something,' dad cried desperately.

'We all want to do something Charlie,' said Sandy quietly and I could see the pain in his eyes. There were thirty men or more milling about the quay and I realised that they were all desperate to help those poor souls on the burning rig. They were all fishermen and any life in danger from the sea needed to be saved in their eyes, no matter who they were or who they worked for.

The door of The Sou' Wester burst open and one of the wives ran out holding a magazine over her head, 'Just got through to the coast guard and they've given their go ahead for us to join the rescue. Three coastguard cutters on the way but two are gonna be two hours at best.'

The fishermen standing around the quay jumped into action immediately. There were to be three small trawlers involved. 'We goin' to need every hand we got,' said Sandy. 'You comin' along?'

Dad swallowed hard before nodding his head determinedly. 'You stay here son, alright?' he said, grasping my shoulder firmly.

'No dad!' I cried. 'I'm coming with you.'

'You're staying here,' was all he said before striding off to one of the boats a group of the village men were already preparing for sea.

I looked around desperately. I wasn't going to let my dad go off into that storm alone, I had to be with him, I knew I could help. The men racing to and fro acted as if I wasn't even there in their frantic haste to get under way. I looked around. The three ships, each about fifteen metres long were moored tight along the quay. The cove itself offered excellent shelter from the enormous waves that could be seen out beyond the peninsula. Inside the harbour there was little more than a heavy swell.

The boat at the front of the three was just casting off and the others were almost ready to follow. A high pitched bark startled me and I looked down to see Fury standing a few metres away. He barked again, turned, ran a few metres and turned again. His dark eyes looked at me intently. I followed without further hesitation and he loped off ahead of me. I realised he was heading to the furthest back of the three trawlers. Three men laboured on deck and another was about to cast off the last rope, tied to the quay at the bow of the boat. Glancing over my shoulder, I saw the first trawler well out into the harbour and heading for the open sea. The second was also pulling away and already twenty metres from the quay. I saw the mooring rope at the front of the last trawler drop into the water and it began to move off, bow first. The trawler men were all consumed with manoeuvring up front and taking a deep breath I launched myself over the side of the quay; I saw dark, cold water below me for a moment before I landed hard on the deck. An instant later, Fury landed heavily beside me, his claws slipping as they fought for purchase on the steel deck.

I smiled, pleased with myself; that lasted for a few moments only, however as it took only that time for the trawler to cross the harbour and pass through the entrance. It was as if some great giant had picked us up and begun to shake us like a toy. The sound of the wind was a constant scream and the waves crashed over the trawler, spraying sheets of icy sea water over me as it was buffeted from side to side.

'What the bloody hell are you doin' here?' a gruff voice said. I was grasped by the scruff of the neck and lifted into the air. A grizzled, beard covered face peered at me. The man was a giant. 'It's young Harry Medhurst ain't it? From the lighthouse? Thought I heard your dad tell you to stay behind. Well, too late now, we can't turn back; and you got that damn mutt with you as well? God help us. Take yourself and the dog below deck before you get washed overboard.' His words were gruff but the keen eyes in his rough face were friendly. He lowered me to the bucking deck and shoved me towards the hatch leading below. I didn't need any more encouragement and calling for Fury to follow, I pulled myself to the hatch. I half fell down the steep steps and Fury landed square on my stomach, winding me for several moments. At last I got my breath back and sat up, soaking, shivering and scared for myself now as well as my dad.

I stumbled along the short corridor and into the crew's quarters. There were two men sitting on the benches smoking. They looked at me in surprise as I held on to a steel column to try and keep from falling as the ship swayed beneath me. Fury stood by my feet, growling softly. 'You look half drowned boy; take a seat and get some tea down to warm you up some.'

I slid onto a bench and accepted a steaming mug one of the men thrust at me. 'I couldn't let my dad go off alone in this storm,' I said, feeling I had to explain my presence there.

'Yeah, well you're here now and you're goin' to have to pitch in if we're to save any of those poor souls on the rig,' the smaller of the two said. 'I'm Jed and this here's Thomas. You're on the Sea Witch. She's my boat and you do what you're told alright?'

'Y...y...yes,' I stammered. 'How long will it take us to get to the Orion V?'

'Not too long,' Jed said frowning. 'I don't think what we find is going to be too pleasant though. I just hope they had enough warning to get off the rig before it went up. The coastguard reckons they'll have a clipper on

163

site in half an hour and we'll be there in about an hour.'

The boat rolled heavily and I was forced to hold on tight as my legs went from under me. Fury was hurled across the cabin and hit the corner of a bench, bolted to the floor, letting out a yelp of pain. He lay panting for a moment before limping into a corner and curling up. I could do nothing but hold on.

Jed threw me a life-jacket which, with great difficulty, I heaved on. Thomas had moved over to the radio and was talking into it urgently and listening intently to what the voice at the other end said in reply. 'The Coast Guard cutter William Cornwallis arrived at the Orion V a few minutes ago. Their captain says it's a real mess. There are helicopters on site as well but they want to know how long until we arrive to lend a hand,' Thomas said, talking to Jed. 'There are men in the water and the captain of the Cornwallis says the sea's on fire.

'Tell him we'll be there in fifteen minutes,' said Thomas. 'Come on boy, we'll need you up on deck before long. We should be able to see what's going on pretty good by now.' With that, Jed grabbed me by the arm and hauled me after him up the stairs I had fallen down such a short time before. Fury limped after me, but Jed yelled, 'you stay there. No place for no damn dog,' and kicked out at Fury who snarled but jumped back a few paces. By the time he had recovered and charged up the steps after me, Jed had swung me through the hatch and slammed it behind him. I could hear Fury's incensed barking even over the storm. 'Here, yelled Jed,' his face only a few inches from mine. 'You keep clipped on to this jackline all the time, d'ya hear?'

I nodded and attached the metal hook to the flat, yellow line that ran all around the trawler. The rain was beating down in sheets and the sea rose and fell in rollercoaster waves. We staggered over to the rail and looked out at what lay ahead. The Sea Witch was just beginning to rise up the next wave, so all I could see was a wall of water until the little trawler topped the wave and there, suddenly, a vision of hell was revealed. The Orion V rig was only about a quarter of a mile away and flames billowed from one side and all around where the helicopter deck was situated. Even at such a distance, the structure was monstrous in size; the great steel legs rose twenty metres out of the water and the highest point on the rig another sixty above that. On the opposite side was the accommodation block. It was not on fire but was wreathed in smoke swept across from the half that was ablaze. The strangest thing was that the sea itself was on fire. The crude oil must have been escaping to the surface where it had caught alight in patches scattered across the heaving waves. The whole scene was bathed in the eerie light of the fires and I couldn't get the sickening thought that there had been dozens of men on the rig when it had gone up out of my mind. How many of them were still alive and how many could be saved? I looked closer and saw that quite a large ship was close to the Orion V, silhouetted by the flames. I knew it must be the Coast Guard ship the William Cornwallis. There were several looping white arcs as hoses on the ship flung water onto the accommodation module. I realised instantly that it was trying to stop the fire engulfing the area where most survivors might be sheltering. I also became aware of searchlights stabbing down from above as several helicopters hovered, directing their lights at the oily sea. They were searching for survivors who had been thrown clear or had jumped to save themselves.

I felt on the verge of panic. How could we, in this shabby little trawler hope to do any good helping in this disaster? As I was thinking, I noticed the other two trawlers that had left before us. They were standing well off from the rig and the Coast Guard cutter, whilst sending cascades of water onto the fire it also pierced the darkness with searchlights flicking across the heaving water. 'They're looking for survivors,' said Jed. 'The report is that six or seven men had to jump into the sea after the first explosion in order to save themselves. They'll be wearing survival suits but it's already best part of an hour since they went in. Got to find them soon or they'll freeze to death.' Over the noise of the storm, I could hear Fury barking frantically behind the closed hatch behind me.

It was hard to imagine that with the surface of the sea on fire and the heat from the burning rig already making my face smart, even from such a distance, that men could freeze to death; but of course, we were talking about the North Atlantic Ocean and even in early June; the water wasn't far above freezing. 'What about the rest of the crew?' I asked.

'Trapped in the accommodation block. They're trying to get the lifeboats to eject but the electrics have gone down. It's a race against time. The fire is being blown in their direction and the William Cornwallis is trying to keep the flames back for as long as possible, but it's just a matter of time before the whole lot goes up. It's a damn dangerous situation.' As he finished speaking there was a mighty explosion from the top of the rig and one of the great cranes perched high on the platform itself swayed lazily before toppling, as if in slow motion into the black sea below. 'I want you to stay in the stern and keep an eye out for survivors in the water. Here, you'll need this if you see anyone.' Jed thrust a long pole with a steel hook on the end into my hands and pushed me towards the stern. 'And keep yourself tied on to the jackline.'

I struggled against the bucking deck and the wind that was trying to fling me over the side. I was shaking with cold and the rain stung my face. Eventually I got to the back of the trawler, where another fisherman was already gazing out at the forbidding sea. I joined him with just a nod at each other, taking the nearest corner and bracing my legs against the steel side of the trawler and a hatch just behind. I strained my eyes but could see no one in the water. I was aware as the trawler turned and the Orion V, burning brightly came into full view that the fire was bigger. That the flames seemed to half engulf the cube of the accommodation block, despite the rain and jets of water cascading down on it from the William Cornwallis. There was another explosion and I felt the shudder through the boat itself. My eyes bulged in astonishment as the monstrous leg supporting the rig closest to us began to buckle. It seemed to cave in and the whole platform above it began to tilt. I was sure the whole rig was going to tip right over and plunge into the sea, taking all those men still trapped inside with it. But accompanied by the anguished rending of metal, the platform came to rest. It must have been leaning at about a twenty five degree angle. It was still there and still burning furiously, but for how much longer I didn't know.

One of the other trawlers crossed our wake and I saw furious activity at the bow as I realised they had spotted a survivor in the water. I saw two men lean over the rail and use a hook similar to mine; even from that distance I could tell one of them was my dad. Heaving hard, a figure slowly emerged from the dark water. It was dressed in a grimy, stained orange survival suit. I saw his hands waving feebly as he reached up desperately. The next moment he had been hauled over the side to safety.

'Look, there!' the fisherman next to me yelled. I tore my eyes away from my father and looked where he was pointing the powerful flashlight. It was difficult to see anything in the rain, wind and boiling sea... but... there, a small speck of orange was it? I peered into the gloom. The fierce beam of the flashlight kept moving about, looking for what it had just picked out of the wild Atlantic, and there it was again; the orange flash, closer this time. It was a man, floating on his back in the murky sea, one arm raised and waving before flopping back into the water. I grabbed the long boat hook and cried, 'Keep the light steady and I'll try to get him.'

As the waves buffeted the trawler, both it and the man were carried on the raging waves, one minute he was only several metres away and the next twenty. Several times I reached out desperately trying to get the hook close enough for the man to grab, but it was so heavy and my arms ached with the effort of wielding it and keeping myself jammed in place against the storm. The man could barely move his arms as the last of his strength was evaporating. He wouldn't last much longer I could tell. I lunged once more and this time my knuckles rapped against the hard steel of the trawlers hull. Letting out a cry of pain, I let go of the boat hook and horrified, watched it cartwheel into the sea. I couldn't take my eyes off the man, I had thrown away any chance of rescuing him... unless... I didn't think, I just knew the man in the water would die unless I acted now. I unhooked the safety line I wore and swung one leg over the side of the trawler. 'Here, what you doin'?' the trawler man at my side shouted in disbelief. I ignored him and pushed myself forward and over the side. The water closed over me like an icy coffin; the breath caught in my throat and there was silence for a moment. I forced my arms to drag me to the surface and the noise of the storm and roaring of the great fire on the rig burst through my senses. Spluttering, I looked around and immediately saw the rig worker's orange survival suit just in front of me. He had lost consciousness and was now floating face down. I swam towards him awkwardly in my lifejacket and grabbed him, turning his body over so his face was out of the water. He looked blue to me and I wasn't sure if he was still breathing. It took all my strength to hold the man on his back; he was big and my legs worked furiously under water, trying to keep him from turning over again. I could feel the icy water chilling me... sucking the life out of me second by second.

I was facing the Sea Witch now but couldn't release my grip on the oil rig survivor in order to grab the boat hook the trawler man I had been standing next to moments before was reaching for me with. The trawler seemed to be getting further away, 'Stop damn you!' I heard him cry, but the words were being blown away from the bridge where the skipper was piloting the boat; he probably didn't even know what was going on at the stern. I watched as the trawler man dashed back towards the hatch to make the rest of the crew aware of my predicament, but my brain, which seemed to be becoming foggy, knew it was all taking far too long. I would be gone and so would the man I was holding long before they could turn the trawler around and come back to me.

As the trawler man yanked the hatch open, the sound of Fury's frenzied barking which had been audible in the background of the storm since I had come on deck got suddenly louder and then Fury was bounding out, past the amazed trawler man and without a moment's hesitation, launched himself over the stern and crashed into the sea. I was finding it hard to keep my legs moving and my eyelids were drooping as the cold crept into my bones. Fury pulled strongly through the angry waves and before I knew it was alongside me, his teeth firmly fixed in my lifejacket. I could feel

171

myself and the unconscious man I grasped being hauled through the churning sea and then the stern of the trawler was looming over me; powerful hands reaching and dragging me from the clutches of the angry ocean. The last thing I remembered before unconsciousness enveloped me was the rough rasp of Fury's tongue as he licked my face.

The rest of what happened out at the Orion V that night I only know through what dad and Jed told me afterwards.

About five minutes after Fury; me and the oil rig worker were saved from the sea, there was a message on the radio. The men trapped on the platform had managed to repair the electrics and were going to turn them on so the lifeboats could be launched. However, there was a good chance that this would ignite more oil on the rig, triggering another explosion. They had to try as the fire was inside the accommodation block by now and the seventy odd men trapped there had only minutes remaining. The Coast Guard cutter William Cornwallis and the three trawlers moved off from the dying rig, to a safe distance. Finally the switch was thrown and the lights came back on all over the rig for a few moments, just long enough for the four, torpedo shaped lifeboats to launch from their tubes and plummet into the sea before more oil on the rig ignited in the biggest fireball so far. The rig had been shaken to its core and slowly toppled and disappeared below the waves, leaving just the stumps of two legs and burning patches of ocean behind it.

All the crew of the rig were saved. It was a miracle some said, others that it showed just how safely the modern rigs were constructed. I knew that every man on that rig should count himself lucky to be alive and the story could just as easily have been that every man had been lost.

Back safely in Peggy's Cove, after I had been checked over by doctors I thought that the whole terrible tale of the Orion V was over. How wrong I was. It was just the beginning.

Part Three
Poison

Chapter 20
Approaching Danger

The following day there were journalists all over Peggy's Cove. There were camera crews around the lighthouse and down by the quay and the phone barely stopped ringing. Dad gave a few interviews, but wouldn't let them talk to me. That was fine as far as I was concerned; after the whole brad Williams and Kent Moon thing I was fed up entirely with being the centre of attention. The news channels were full of the story and there were live feeds from Dartmouth where the survivors from the Orion V had been taken. There were also pictures of the ruins of the rig, looking sad and desolate; just a few pieces of twisted metal sticking out of the ocean now the storm had passed.

I didn't watch much of it and turned the TV off straight after the report on the rescue of the oil rig's crew. I managed to escape in the early afternoon. I crept past the massed group of reporters and ran down the peninsula with Fury at my heels.

The storm had cleared the air and there was a real feel of spring in the mild temperature and newly budding flowers and trees. I hadn't been over to Cranberry Cove for a couple of days because of the storm and as I strode towards The Sanctuary I was amazed at how much debris had piled up on the shore. There was wood, plastic bottles and a wide variety of other flotsam that had travelled the seas.

Gabe and Jen were sitting at the kitchen table. Molly was there as well with Stella perched on her shoulder, whiskers twitching inquisitively. I smiled warmly at her. 'Hi,' I said.

'Hi yourself,' replied Molly. 'Hear you were a bit of a hero out at the rig last night.'

'I wouldn't say that. And I nearly drowned.' I said embarrassed.

'We're really proud of you,' said Jen.

I could feel myself blushing. As I looked at the three of them, I realised that they seemed a bit subdued. 'Is everything alright?' I asked.

'Everything's all right just now, but it won't be soon, it'll be absolute hell soon,' said Gabe with a loud sigh.

I was confused by Gabe's words. 'I don't understand,' I said. 'What's going to happen?'

Gabe waved his arm in the direction of the Atlantic Ocean, 'The Orion V rig blowing up last night was a disaster and it was almost a miracle that every man was rescued, but they'd already struck the oil hadn't they; been pumping it out for the last few weeks. Only now the rigs gone; but the oil's still pumping out of the seabed; thousands of gallons an hour probably; straight into the ocean. And the trouble with crude oil is that it floats, and what floats follows the currents and that means all that crude oil is going to end up here on the coast of Nova

176

Scotia. Might take a day or two but it'll get here and when it does, it's going to kill near every living wild creature it comes into contact with.

I looked at Gabe aghast, 'Are you sure?' I managed to ask.

'It's going to happen,' said Jen calmly. 'We've seen it before, when we were in Alaska; The Exxon Valdez oil spill. You've never seen anything like it. The whole coastline for miles around, covered in that disgusting, stinking mess and as you walked along, seeing lumps that when you poked, you realised were birds, or seals or any one of a dozen types of animal, dead and covered in that poisonous filth.'

'Didn't anything survive?' I asked, horrified.

'Some,' Jen said quietly. 'Those we found early enough or that were not too badly covered. But it was always touch and go and such a hard, long job to clean and treat each and every one.'

'We need to prepare,' said Gabe. 'There'll be a lot of support to fight the pollution eventually, but most of it will come too late. If we can be ready from the start, we'll save more. Are you two going to join us?'

Molly and I looked at each other. Of course we were going to help and I suspected most of the population of Peggy's Cove and beyond would as well.

We listened to the news constantly from that moment on. The story of the survival of the Orion V's crew had quickly faded as the new risk to Canada became apparent. Reports on the oil slick that was forming told a worrying story of what was to come. By two days after the Orion V fire, the slick was five miles long. The weather was calm and windless so it had stayed roughly in the same position. However, the forecast for the following few days was for more unsettled weather and stronger winds blowing on-shore. This would drive the oil slick onto the coast of Nova Scotia.

The oil company, the Canadian government and several environmental agencies were all working to try and disperse the oil before it reached land, but ships, personnel and chemicals all had to be brought to Nova Scotia and they weren't there yet. The oil company was working to seal the escaping oil from the sea-bed but that would take at least three days, and all the time the oil was escaping and the slick growing.

I stood on the beach in front of The Sanctuary at Cranberry Cove with Molly beside me. We both gazed out across the Atlantic. The distant shape of the Orion V rig had gone now of course and the sea looked its normal bluey grey. Yet, we both knew that the oil slick was out there somewhere, getting closer by the minute. 'How are things at home?' I asked.

'Awful,' Molly replied. Stella was skipping around our feet, splashing in and out of the waves and chasing her tail. Fury sat by my feet, watching the otter with head tilted. 'He's angry all the time now, since the oil company withdrew its decision to buy the properties round here. He's stuck with me in Peggy's Cove and he doesn't like it. Drinks all the time, never works and takes any opportunity to pick a fight with me. I wish he would just disappear.' There was a terrible sadness in Molly's voice and I felt my heart want to break at the thought of how hard life was for her and how she must feel.

'Couldn't you move in here, at The Sanctuary for a while? Just whilst we see what happens with the slick.'

'I've already asked Jen. She said that would be fine if and when the oil gets here.'

'What if it doesn't?' I asked. 'What if they get it cleared up before it reaches land? You can't stay living with that man. He should be in prison and you should be happy.'

Molly turned her head and smiled sadly at me, 'I'm happy enough when I'm here. And both Gabe and Jen think the efforts to get rid of the oil at sea will come to nothing.'

We both looked at the landscape around us; it was beautiful with the crisp, grey, white rocks and pine forests reaching back to the rolling hills beyond. Just along the bay there were seals laying on the shore and sea birds circling above. It was a haven for all sorts of wildlife and I couldn't believe that anything could really happen to change that.

Chapter 21
Black Tide

The next day, the second after the Orion V disaster, the operation to disperse the oil slick began. We listened to its progress on the radio and watched from the shore at Cranberry Cove. Initially several large ships appeared and later in the day, a fleet of smaller boats, fitted with wide steel arms stretching far out began to join in. The larger ships began to lay floating booms to try and trap the oil, keeping it in one place whilst the smaller ships sailed back and forth spraying tonne after tonne of detergent on the thick crude oil in an attempt to break it up and sink it to the ocean floor. 'Everything they do is poisoning the sea,' Gabe said sadly. 'The crude oil is the worst, but the detergent is nearly as bad. Who knows how much marine life has died already due to the oil and detergents. And it won't work. It didn't back when the Exxon Valdez ran aground and it won't this time.'

We listened to the news and watched the sea with bated breath.

The attempt to clean up the crude oil carried on through the night. It was still far out at sea but even the small boats spraying detergent were visible through binoculars; dozens of bright lights swaying to and fro in the distance. By the time I went to bed that night, with Fury lying beside me, I felt some hope that the government and the oil company combined might beat the slick before it reached us.

The phone rang at half past four in the morning and as I slept on the sofa, I had the receiver in my hand before the third ring; it was Jen Munroe, 'Oh God Harry, it's here. You need to come straight away and call for Molly on your way.' She had put the receiver down before I could say anything.

There was just the first glimmer of sunlight on the horizon as I reached the steps to Molly's house. Fury wouldn't go up them, but just stayed by the bottom step growling softly. I hammered on the door. A shambling figure approached and the peeling door was wrenched open 'oow' are yer?' the voice demanded. The bloated face, framed by long greasy hair and at least a week of dark stubble on its chin leered as the sunken, piggy eyes focussed on me. 'Well, if it ain't lover boy. Know who you've come for, but it's the middle of the night. What you want with my Moll?'

I gritted my teeth as I forced myself to speak to this creature, 'The oil slicks hit the shore. She's needed to help with injured animals.'

'Injured animals?' he slurred at me, clearly drunk, 'She ain't helping no bloody animals. She's staying here and cleaning the house is what she's doing, when she gets up.' There was a movement behind this horrible man and in the gloom I could just make out Molly, tip-toeing down the stairs, pulling her old coat on as she went. 'Now, boy, you just clear off, an' I don't wanna see ya round here no more.' He suddenly lunged forward, pretending to grab me; I leapt backwards, stumbling down the porch steps, but Fury was up past me, barking madly and snapping at the man. Molly's step-father gave a terrified cry and slammed the door closed before Fury could get to him.

'Come on!' a voice called and I saw Molly run from the back of the house where she had got out without her drunken step-father knowing.

I called Fury, and with an indignant snort, he followed as we ran to join Molly. We didn't stop to talk, we just ran as fast as we could, through Peggy's Cove and on towards Cranberry Cove. I looked into the harbour as we passed but there was no sign of the brown poison there.

When we reached Cranberry Cove, I was relieved to see that it was clear as well, except for... what was that brown splodge on the shore? We went to investigate. Fury ran ahead, but as he reached the shape, he shrank back and began circling it cautiously at a distance. As we got closer, we could see that it was a sea bird. It looked like it was originally white, but it was hard to tell now as it was stained brown with streaks of thick crude oil clinging to it. The poor thing was obviously dead. We were both saddened by the sight of that poor lifeless body, but there were no others. As we trudged on, I did notice the odd patch of oil coating a few of the rocks right where the Atlantic waves rolled in. I frowned and looked out to sea, but there was nothing visible, apart from the growing fleet of boats and ships joining in the clean-up around the vanished oil rig.

At The Sanctuary, we found Gabe and Jen in the kitchen. With newspapers spread all over the table, Gabe held a big sea bird steady as Jen used a swab to clean the oil coating its feathers. 'It's a Northern Gannet isn't it?' said Molly. She turned to me and added, 'The same as the one we saw on the beach.'

This one was alive, but it was barely moving. The oil was concentrated around its wings and the underside of its body. 'It probably drifted into some of the oil floating on the surface, but took off before it got completely covered.'

'Will it be alright?' I asked.

Gabe looked at me with sad eyes, 'It might pull through. Depends how much it swallowed and if it breathed much in. Crude oil burns the lungs and poisons the blood system, and of course, once it gets onto their feathers, they try to clean themselves and more of it gets inside them. The oil clogs their feathers and either they tire with the extra weight and drown or it sticks the feathers together so they can't work properly to keep them warm and they die of hypothermia.'

'But you got this one in time didn't you?' I continued.

'Maybe,' said Gabe. 'We'll clean it up, keep it safe and feed it. Just have to keep our fingers crossed. And we can't release it until the whole spill is cleared up or it'll just get oiled up all over again.'

'Is this the first?' asked Molly.

'There are three others that we have already cleaned up,' said Jen. 'They were rescued by people out walking late last night and dropped round to us this morning by the state police.'

'But when you rang, I thought the oil was on the beaches,' I said. I felt annoyed that they had panicked me over a couple of birds when I had been expecting so much worse.

'It is here,' said Jen in a cold voice. 'This is the beginning. The government and the oil company haven't managed to stop the oil, and more is still pumping out from the sea floor. There's nothing we can do to stop it now.'

'What will happen then?' asked Molly in a quiet voice.

'Then, Molly, beautiful wild creatures will die. And our stunning coastline will be stained for years to come,' said Gabe.

'But, what are the government going to do about it?' I said.

'To start with... Not much. If they were prepared for something like this, there would be a dozen clean-up and veterinary centres set up along this coast already. But there's just us.' Jen put down the cloth she had been using to clean the sorry looking gannet. 'Eventually they'll get everything in place and a lot of volunteers too, but it's right now we need it. Go and see if there's any change outside will you? I've got to put this little fella away to recover.'

'Okay,' I said. Molly and I made our way back outside. We had probably only been in The Sanctuary for half an hour, but the change we saw took my breath away. The sun was just beginning to rise and the first rays of sunlight fell on a scene straight out of a horror movie. It was like the whole cove had caught a terrible disease. The crude oil had finally arrived and it was like a dirty blanket that smothered the sea. The shoreline was covered in it and it clung tenaciously to everything it touched. And the stink, it was so strong I felt like being sick; the smell of petrol but thicker, it almost seemed to coat your tongue as you breathed it in. It took a few more seconds before I began to notice strange mounds on the beach. They weren't rocks, there were none there. With a sickening feeling in the pit of my stomach I lurched forward. I had to see what they were.

By the time I reached the nearest mound, about the size of a rubbish sack, my feet and trousers were already caked in the filthy crude oil. I fell to my knees and, placing one hand on the shape, tried to wipe the oil away. An eye stared up at me, unseeing and lifeless. I felt tears well up in my own eyes. It was a grey seal; the same as I had seen alive and well the day before. Now it was dead, killed by this terrible poison. There were four other similar sized mounds beneath the fetid, stinking oil and still more off in the distance around the bay; but they weren't the only ones. There were smaller shapes, visible in the sticky mess, and they were more easily recognisable as birds; just as dead and more of them.

'This can't be happening!' Molly cried from behind me. As I turned, I saw her with her hands to her mouth, tears streaming from her eyes. Fury was rubbing himself against her legs as if trying to comfort her and they both stood just beyond the oil as if they were scared it would burn them.

'It is happening Molly,' I said, 'and we've got to start doing something to help. I took her hand and led her slowly back towards The Sanctuary. I tried not to look at the shapes along the shoreline; more and more of them were visible as the sun rose and the scale of this disaster was only just starting to dawn on me..

'Oh, what about Stella?' Molly suddenly cried. 'I've got to see if she's alright.' Without another word, Molly ran off. I let her go. I knew how much that beautiful, graceful little creature meant to her. Stella was how Molly escaped from her real life; from the beatings and abuse that she suffered almost every day. I could feel my blood begin to boil of the thought of what Molly had to put up with; I would do something about it I promised myself for probably the hundredth time; but not now, not today. Right now I had to help with the disaster that was unfolding around me.

The next few hours were a blur. The phone rang almost constantly in The Sanctuary. People who were out for early morning walks, rangers, police; anyone who came close to the ocean within a few miles was ringing. They were finding oil covered birds and marine mammals stranded on the beaches and rocks, covered in thick crude oil. The calls that came in were all about those creatures found alive; but each caller talked in shocked tones of the dozens, hundreds of others they had seen dead.

As the first poor creatures arrived, we set up a simple system to deal with them; two trestle tables joined on to the kitchen table, bowls of water, plastic bottles of detergent, coarse brushes and towels. As each animal arrived, Gabe or Jen assessed its condition. If it was possible to save it came to me to start the cleaning. The most heart-breaking thing of all was that those that had swallowed too much or were too weak or damaged had to be put down. They would have died slow deaths if they were just left; Gabe put them out of their pain with a simple injection. They slipped away peacefully but tears rolled down our faces each time it happened. Molly and I had to focus on those that could be saved - Molly had returned after being reassured that her beloved Stella was safe and sound, locked in The Water Park - and the first step was to clean off any excess oil with a scrapper. The oil that came off, we scraped into a big bucket, trying not to hurt the delicate creatures.

Once the worst of the oil was removed, we started using rags and detergent to clean off as much of the remaining oil as possible. It was a long, slow job and when as much oil as possible had been removed; the animal was put into a cage in one of the sheds to recover. They would need yet more cleaning later.

We carried on this cleaning for hour after hour. By late morning four of the other regular volunteers had turned up. They joined our cleaning team and it became a bit like a production line. We got better with each new patient, but the number of patients was rising. There were already a dozen birds waiting their turn and oil was beginning to smear almost every surface in the now crowded kitchen.

By late afternoon we were all exhausted and there were over a hundred birds, two seals and a sea lion waiting in the courtyard.

We listened to the radio constantly and it told the unfolding story of the oil reaching different parts of the coastline for ten miles east and west of us throughout the day. The dreadful toll of wildlife killed by the poisonous oil rose rapidly into the thousands and the numbers were just so huge they seemed almost meaningless. Interviews with outraged people from various agencies; deploring the lack of resources to save the wildlife; pleas to save the tourist industry, the livelihoods of local people who depended on the sea. And we could vouch for their concern. We were on our knees, totally overwhelmed by the endless and increasing rate that oil covered, dying creatures were being brought to our door. The pile of dead birds and mammals in the yard was a small hill now and growing hour by hour. I was filled with horror at the number and range of creatures that were falling victim to this terrible calamity that had befallen our beautiful land. But it was beautiful no longer; it was black, brown, dirty, stained and smelt of death. The tears just wouldn't stop rolling down my cheeks and whenever I looked up it was into the red-rimmed eyes of Molly whose fingers were bleeding from the effort she was putting into the scrubbing of the poor helpless creatures that passed one after the other through her hands.

Two days it went on like that. It seemed like a dream. a conveyor belt of sick animals, gasping for breath, their lungs, skin, feathers, blood, contaminated by the black poison. There was no shortage of volunteers after the first day; almost everyone in Peggy's Cove had come to help at one time or another, but there was only so much detergent, only so many cages to hold the poorly cleaned animals once we had finished. They came and helped though and it gave me time to see Fury who wouldn't move from outside the kitchen door whilst I was inside. I didn't have to call mum and dad, because they turned up to help late on the first day, with Sal as well. There was a small fleet of cars acting like taxis. The few beds at The Sanctuary couldn't cope with the sudden influx of people so the cars were used to ferry the townsfolk back to their homes for a few hours sleep before returning to the battle. Most people wanted to stay no matter what but Jen and Gabe convinced them they would soon become useless if exhaustion overtook them. They had to have some sleep even if it was just a few hours if they were to save as many of the poisoned animals as they could.

The detergent ran out at the end of the second day and there was still no sign of the government or the oil company helping. It was all taking just too long and in the meantime, wild animals in their thousands were dying.

We snatched brief spells of sleep here and there throughout the second night. I took Fury out for a walk back into the forest, away from the smell of the oil and the feeling of death that cloaked the coast right up to the high tide line. The breeze was blowing from the hills, so the fresh scent of pine and clean air filled my lungs. Molly had refused to come with me, preferring to sit in 'The Water Park' playing with her beloved Stella, who must have been going stir crazy, locked in what for an otter would be considered a tiny space.

I was only away for an hour, but when I returned, things had changed. A new supply of detergent had been delivered by The Royal Canadian Mounted Police no less and there was almost a party spirit as the radio had announced that the government had at last got itself into gear and treatment centres to deal with oil polluted animals were being set up all along the coast.

I can't say that the end was in sight then as the oil was still on the beaches and animals were still dying in terrible numbers, but the tide began to turn from that moment.

As a registered animal rescue charity, The Sanctuary became the local centre for treating animals suffering the effects of the oil spill. Lorries of supplies and coaches of volunteers flooded in. Very soon there were large, canvas army tents erected along the track leading back from The Sanctuary itself towards the highway.

The huge pile of dead animals was taken away and the remains burnt to avoid further contamination. I couldn't watch them load the sad looking bodies into trucks; it was just too awful after all the death I had faced in the last forty eight hours. I busied myself with the living, with the creatures still alive and with a fighting chance of survival.

Things became much more organised. There were several more vets on site and a company of soldiers organising and doing all the heavy work. Gabe said there were nine other centres set up along the affected stretch of coast now. But no sign of the oil company; not a single person, not a single resource, and gee, were people angry about it.

Molly and I slept in sleeping bags in a little loft room at the top of The Sanctuary. We had slept there often before. I was surprised Molly was in such high spirits when we zipped ourselves in to our bags for two hours sleep late on the third night, 'How are you coping?' I asked.

'Alright,' she replied. 'I feel awful for the animals of course; that's heart-breaking, obviously.'

'I feel like crying all the time,' I said quietly. 'But there are times when I look at you at the moment and I could almost think you looked happy.'

Molly looked at me for a long time before replying, 'I could count on one hand the number of days I haven't cried in the last three years,' she said, her voice quaking slightly.

I felt ashamed of myself. Here was I, with a happy life - not now, but generally - and my poor friend here lived a life of constant misery. Her parents were dead, her step-father was a monster. Every day must have been an unbelievable struggle to get through.

'The thing is,' Molly said, lowering her eyes, 'here, right now, I'm with kind people who like me. When I go to sleep here, I feel safe, I get fed proper food made by someone who asks me what I want; and most importantly of all, I'm with my best friends.'

I screwed my face up in confusion.

Molly smiled shyly, 'You, Fury and Stella you idiot.' She looked unhappy again, like she normally did. 'But sometime soon it'll all go back to how it was, how it really is.'

I didn't know what to say for a few moments. 'I will get you away from that man,' I whispered. 'I promised you before and I meant it.'

She reached out her hand and briefly squeezed mine, before turning over and huddling into her sleeping bag. I knew she didn't believe me. That she appreciated my words but thought they were just that; words.

It had been the middle of the third night when we grabbed those hours of sleep. We woke to the dawn of the fourth day after the oil came ashore and dragged ourselves downstairs. The battle to save the damaged and slime coated creatures continued unabated. We threw ourselves back into the relentless cleaning after a quick mug of sweet tea and a slice of thick buttered toast. Ma was manning the kitchen now, making sure the army of volunteers were fed and watered regularly.

'I'm going to see Stella,' Molly said during our first break after three hours soaping a variety of sea birds with detergent. I just nodded.

The scream came a minute later and I knew it was Molly instantly. I wrapped the gull, whose wings I had almost completely cleaned of oil, in a thick towel so it couldn't move, put it down carefully and ran out of the tent I had been working in. I saw Molly off by herself, just outside 'The Water Park'. She had her hands held to her face and was wailing uncontrollably.

'What's the matter?' I yelled, taking her by the elbow.

She turned and looked at me, her hands now holding the sides of her head. Her eyes were wild, 'She's gone!' she cried. 'Stella's gone.'

Chapter 22
Race Against Time

Looking closely, I saw there was a hole in the bottom of the wooden door to what had been the pantry. I stepped forward and looked at it more carefully. There were teeth marks where the wood was splintered. Stella had gnawed her way out. She may have been raised as a pet by Molly, but she still had the desire to be free and out in the great, wide world.

Molly had slumped to the floor; her sobs shook her whole, frail little body. 'She'll die,' Molly said through the tears. 'She'll get covered in that awful oil and die a horrible death. She'll drown or die of hypothermia or the stuff will poison her blood. What am I going to do?'

'I'll find her,' I said firmly. 'Don't you worry; I'll find her and bring her back safe and sound.'

'Will you? Will you really?' asked Molly, the desperation clear in her voice.

'I will,' I said. 'I'll take Fury.' Molly got unsteadily to her feet and began to follow me. 'No, you stay here. We'll move more quickly on our own.' Molly looked about to argue but then just nodded. I couldn't ask anyone else to go with me, they were all so consumed in saving the steady stream of poisoned creatures arriving at The Sanctuary. I would have to find Stella with just Fury to help.

Once outside, I called Fury and he came running. 'We've got to find Stella,' I said. Fury looked up at me quizzically. 'Come with me,' I said and with Fury trotting behind I went back to 'The Water Park', where I beckoned Fury to the hole Stella had made. He nosed at it tentatively, snorting deeply before barking loudly twice. Without another word from me, Fury turned and ran. I picked up the rucksack I had quickly packed and followed him.

It was difficult to keep up, Fury was powerful and fast, but every hundred yards or so he stopped and peered back, waiting till I got within ten metres before bounding off again. In half an hour, we must have been at least two miles from The Sanctuary, travelling along the tree-line a hundred metres or so back from the shore. It was hard going, but Fury seemed to have Stella's scent and I was pleased, but surprised that the otter had not just headed straight for the sea.

I didn't know exactly where we were, but remembered that there was an estuary a couple of bays along from Cranberry Cove, where a river met the sea. Instantly it clicked; Stella was a freshwater otter and though she swam in the sea, it was fresh water that she craved. After having been cooped up for four days, she had finally had enough and was making for the river. I felt some hope rise within me. Maybe she had stayed away from the coast and the poisonous crude oil. Maybe she would be swimming in the fresh water of the river estuary where the oil hadn't reached. Maybe I really could save her.

I could feel the tiredness that a couple of hours sleep had kept at bay come back like a tidal wave. My legs were leaden and I was finding it hard to keep my mind on the search. I had already run close to two miles and I was gasping for breath. The ground rose ahead of us and I could see Fury standing at the top of the low ridge looking back at me. With a final effort, I pulled myself up the slope, grasping handfuls of grass to pull myself up. Eventually I fell, panting to the ground as the slope evened out.

On all fours, my lungs burning, I looked over the ridge and saw the river estuary stretched out before me. The river widened here, where it met the sea and it must have been a couple of hundred metres from the bank, some fifty metres way at the bottom of the slope to the opposite bank. This was where the fresh water of the river met the salt water of the Atlantic Ocean. Over to my left, the estuary opened out even further as it joined the great ocean and the river ceased to exist. I noticed a small island, nearly in the centre of the estuary, just about where I thought the river finally became the Atlantic Ocean. If I was going to find Stella, this is where she would be. As I gradually got my breath back, I grabbed the binoculars from my rucksack. Fury was rushing from side to side on the flat rocks below; nose to the ground as he searched for Stella's scent. He had clearly lost it on the hard, bare rock. I scanned the ground ahead in slow sweeps, finally looking at the river in minute detail. There was very little sign of life; even birds were visibly missing, what with the number poisoned by the oil spill.

I could feel fear begin to clutch at my heart. What if I couldn't find the otter? I knew what Stella meant to Molly and I was really worried how she would take it if Stella was gone for good, or worse yet... dead. There... there! A small dot was visible far out in the estuary, and I knew it was the smooth aquiline head of that little otter. Taking the binoculars away from my eyes for a minute, I looked where she was. The relief I had momentarily felt melted away, to be replaced by a cold dread. Stella was heading out towards the sea, towards the little island in the middle of the estuary. I had no idea why she was going there, but she was and that was where the oil was. Here, within the estuary, the fresh water was flowing out, keeping the poisonous oil away, but out there, where the fresh water mixed with the salty Atlantic, death waited and the little otter was swimming straight into it.

Fury barked once and I saw him dashing off towards the river, having once more picked up Stella's scent. But I knew where she was.

Wearily, I stood and stumbled down the slope and across the bare rock. I halted at the edge of the estuary; the water looked muddy and fast flowing, but clear of any sign of oil. I had a moment of indecision, but I knew I had to save Stella for Molly. I threw my jacket onto the ground and tightened the straps on my small rucksack. With trepidation, I stepped into the river. The current pulled at my legs instantly and by the time I was in to my knees, the cold was already taking my breath away. This was stupid, I knew it, but I kept on. Fury was barking manically at me; he wanted me to stop; he realised how foolish and dangerous my actions were. I didn't stop though, I waded forward and when the water was waist high, I threw myself forward and began to swim strongly for the island that must have been about three hundred metres away.

I moved fast through the water, Fury's barking fading into the distance before stopping altogether. I tried not to swallow the brown river water, keeping my head well up. I could feel my muscles tightening as the cold slowly drained the heat from my body. It might only have been three hundred metres, but It seemed to take an age to get halfway. It was only then that I became aware of a snorting behind me. Looking over my shoulder, I was astonished to see Fury paddling determinedly. I cursed myself for not realising he would follow me. I should have tied him up on the bank, but it was too late for that; I concentrated on getting to the island.

I was still fifty metres away from the island when I saw to my horror that the rocks where it emerged from the water were slick with oil. The dark brown scum clung to the island as if trying to drag it down. And then I was in the oil myself. I began to panic. It was thick and clung to my skin. I stretched my head as high up as possible to keep the poison from my mouth and eyes. 'Oh God!' I cried in despair as I realised that Fury, paddling hard behind me would be coated in the oil as well, and he didn't know how dangerous it was. I turned with difficulty in the thick soup and paddled back towards Fury whose head was only five metres behind. 'Go back!' I cried desperately, but of course he just kept coming, his great dark eyes fixed on me. Then he hit the oil. His great head shook in confusion and I saw the crude oil clinging to his fur. I lunged forward and grasped his muzzle, forcing his head up. Fury didn't panic, he kept paddling, allowing me to keep his head up and well away from the stinking oil. I had to swim on my back now and the oil filled my hair and slopped across my face as I struggled to keep Fury's head up and swim with one hand. My head submerged once and I was at once covered in the dense, poisonous crude. I coughed and kept my eyes tight shut. I trod water for a moment and desperately wiped at my eyes with my only free hand. When I opened my eyes, they stung madly and burned, but I had to carry on. I could make out the rocky shore of the island just a few metres away and then felt rock beneath my feet. I stumbled to get my balance, but as soon as I did, I pulled Fury up and dragged him onto the oil covered rocks of the island. I kept edging backwards until we were both far enough that we were above the water line.

I just lay there, shivering; my backpack digging into me as I lay panting. Fury lay at my side, his fur clogged with oil. I kept tight hold of his head so he couldn't lick himself.

It took a good ten minutes for me to stop shaking and regain my breath. I had to let go of Fury and he managed to sit up. He looked forlornly down at his ruined fur but didn't try to lick it. Unsteadily, I stood and looked around me. It was time to find Stella. I had already realised the little otter must have swum through the oil slick herself, and being lower in the water, would have been completely coated in the stuff. I wanted to stay positive but I realised there was little hope she would be alive.

My clothes were soaked and I was coated in crude oil. My eyes were clogged and I had swallowed some of the stuff as well. My eyes burned and I felt sick. I lay my rucksack down and began to explore the little island. It couldn't have been more than about thirty metres across, mainly made up of bare, white rock with a few trees and shrubs on the flattened top. I was really worried then. I had been unbelievably foolish in swimming out there to rescue Stella and now Fury was coated in the poisonous crude and I didn't know how I was going to get him back to shore, especially against the current of the fresh water flowing out of the estuary.

'Stay here Fury,' I said and he sank down onto the cold rock, shivering. I clambered over the rocks, looking into every nook and cranny. The top of the island was fairly flat with some soil and a handful of pine trees. It was here that I saw the little body. It was lying on its side, the fur matted with the thick crude oil that coated it. The mouth was open and I knew instantly that it was dead. I felt tears well up, making my eyes burn even more; I must have cried out because my sobs were suddenly interrupted by a soft rustle in a bush close by and a dark shape appeared from under it. It was another otter, covered in oil, but alive. It crept out, taking a few unsteady paces with its short legs before collapsing on the carpet of pine needles. I went over, trying to wipe the tears from my eyes without blinding myself even more with oil. I bent down to inspect the newcomer. Imagine my shock and surprise when I realised I was looking at Stella. She must have followed the dead otter out there, desperate for the company of her own kind; she was covered in the filthy crude oil but her bright eyes were looking at me as her mouth opened and closed, gasping for breath. I fell to my knees and carefully scooped the otter up; she was quite heavy now, a metre long and covered in oil. I staggered to my feet and stumbled back to the rocky shore. Fury whined as I virtually fell down the steep slope and dropped to my knees beside him.

I lay Stella before me and had to stop Fury from trying to lick the otter as she just lay there, too poorly to move. I unzipped my rucksack and pulled out some old cloths and a small bottle of detergent. I knew I didn't have enough to clean Stella properly, but there might be enough to get the worst of it off from around her head so she didn't lick anymore and add to the poison already in her frail little body. She just lay there as I wiped the detergent soaked cloth over her fur. It took half an hour before I had got the worst of the oil off, down to her neck. The rest of her was still clogged with oil and she refused to move; her bright little eyes stared at me all the time though and that was enough to make me believe I had a chance.

I had to rest after cleaning Stella and I began to think about what to do next. It was a very dangerous situation I was in and in order to rescue Stella, I had also put the life of my dearest friend, Fury in the balance.

There were moments in the next couple of hours when I just wanted to give up. I couldn't think how to get myself, Fury and Stella back to the shore and then to the safety of Cranberry Cove. I wracked my brains with no success. I had no more tears to shed but I felt such a deep sadness at the thought of both Fury and Stella losing their lives out here on this lonely little island that it was almost too much to bear.

When it came, the idea seemed absurd and I wasn't even sure if I was thinking straight. It was still only mid afternoon, but there was a faint outline of the moon already visible. And there it was, the idea; the moon was responsible for the tides and this river must be a tidal river, which meant that when the tide came in, the flow of water at the surface would reverse as water from the ocean forced its way back up the channel. At that moment, there might be an opportunity to make for the shore and not be swept out to sea. But if the sea water moved up stream, it would carry the oil with it, wouldn't it? I reasoned. What if I managed to get past the oil around the island (it was only about ten metres wide here at the moment) and tried to stay ahead of the incoming oil on the tide? It might work, but it would need precise timing and a lot of luck. Stella was going nowhere under her own steam and Fury would find swimming very difficult with the weight of all that oil in his fur; it would drag him down and he could easily drown. I on the other hand was pretty fit on the whole; covered in oil, feeling queasy and eyes burning, but generally okay.

I kept mulling the idea over, trying to work out how to get us all to shore. I could leave Fury and Stella of course and come back for help, but Stella would never survive that long; I didn't want to leave Fury either. The oil had obviously only just reached this far as it wasn't already polluting the banks of the river upstream, but that would change after the high tide. The whole estuary would be drowned in the vile poison. Then how would I rescue Fury? And who would come back and help me? Every pair of hands was already full with saving the lives of oiled up animals arriving at the treatment centres, without anyone waltzing off with me to try and save one dog and an otter. I had to take them with me.

By about five I had come up with a plan. I guessed that the moon would be overhead in about an hour and that would be high tide. I would have to watch carefully to judge exactly the moment to go; if I mistimed it, we would either get swept out to sea or caught in the oil as it overran the estuary with the incoming tide.

I had seen a large piece of driftwood on the seaward side of the island, thrown up onto the rocks by a storm sometime in the past. It was about two metres long, bleached white and shaped like a letter 'L'. It was about the thickness of my thigh at its widest. I managed to drag it up and over the island until it lay on the shore just above the film of oil lapping at the discoloured rock. I used my knife to cut my rucksack into strips of material and tied several of them together. I then used these improvised lengths of rope to tie Stella to the top of the log; she just lay there, looking at me. I used some of the oil covered cloths to pad her, so the straps didn't hurt. The final length of rope was to tie Fury to the log with, but that would have to be right as we started our escape bid. I had mulled over how to tell the exact moment to depart and I now sat with a small pile of twigs at the end of the island closest to the shore we would be making for and also where the flow of water would be fastest, without the mass of the island to hinder it. Every minute, I tossed a twig out over the oil, onto the open water and watched to see what happened to it. So far every twig had been carried out towards the sea and been engulfed in the oil.

For another half an hour I sat, throwing the sticks and watching. It was nearly six and the light was beginning to fade. I crossed my fingers tightly; I really didn't want to attempt the crossing in the dark.

With one hand I stroked Stella's head as she lay, tied to the log. Fury just sat, shivering, looking from me to the young otter. With the oil in their fur, I knew that both animals would be losing heat more quickly and that would only speed up once we got into the water. I threw another twig, almost without thinking and it took me a minute to realise that this one had not drifted out towards the sea but was just sitting there. Even as I watched, it began to float ever so slowly back towards the river estuary. The tide was turning. It was now or never. I had to get in the water fast or the oil would overtake us.

'Wait!' I shouted at Fury as I leapt to my feet and hauled the log into the oil covered water. It rolled slightly, finding its centre of gravity and for a moment I thought it was going to roll over completely, submerging Stella, but it stopped and rolled back slightly. I manhandled the log out, until I was knee deep in the icy water, the oil making my hands slick and slippery. 'Come on Fury!' I called and the magnificent creature rose slowly. I could tell he didn't want to go back into the oil so I coaxed him with as soft a voice as I could manage. Fury ambled down the rocky shore and into the oil coated water. He immediately put his muzzle down and I reached out quickly to keep it out of the poisonous crude oil. I had to drag him further in, and as soon as he was alongside the log, I pulled out the rope and looped it round the dog and the log together, tying it as best I could with hands that could barely grip in the treacherous oil. By the time I had finished, and looked out over the estuary, I could tell that we were very nearly too late. The tide was moving in faster now and the oil slick was past the island by several meters already. I had to get ahead of it if we were not to drown in that awful, clawing mess.

With one hand stretched over the log and Fury's back, I kicked off, gasping as the cold struck my body. I tried to keep my head up but my feet slipped and my head went under. I choked on a mouthful of crude oil and retched violently. I wiped my face as quickly as I could before using my free arm and legs to strike out from the island. We had to get through the edge of the oil slick and stay ahead of it as it rounded the island and was carried onwards upstream to spread yet more pollution.

Fury was kicking strongly now that he had got used to being tied to the log. He seemed to realise the urgency of the situation and I saw his eyes fixed on the shore, still three hundred metres away. It was hard going, the oil was thick as porridge and every movement was a strain. For long minutes, I didn't think we were going to make it, when suddenly, the log broke free of the oil slick and we were in muddy but oil free water. It was a little easier then, and we began to pull ahead of the oil, which was advancing on the incoming tide.

Three hundred metres doesn't sound very far; you could run it in a minute or so, but in the icy waters of the Atlantic, tired, hauling a log, an otter and a dog, it could have been ten miles. Fury was beginning to tire and the log was tipping as Fury's sodden, oil soaked fur began to pull him down. I had to start supporting the dog's weight and keep above the water. Fury's kicking was becoming ragged and I was devoting so much more effort into keeping him up that I couldn't help move us forward.

We were at the mercy of the current and that would just carry us upriver rather than to the nearest shore. In desperation, I pulled myself to the front of the log. With my left arm, I grabbed the 'L' part of the log, which rose out of the water and used my body weight to pull it down. As it tipped, Fury, whose body was on the opposite side, rose slightly in the water. I lay back and kicked as hard as I could with my free hand and legs. Fury found a renewed energy and his legs worked harder as his wild eyes, full of fear now looked at me.

I was gasping for breath, a stitch like a white hot needle lancing through my side. But I gritted my teeth and kept kicking. With my head back, I couldn't see what progress we were making, but I did know I wouldn't be able to keep this up for much longer. The pain in my muscles was excruciating and Fury was completely exhausted, his legs, barely moving. There was white spittle at the corners of his mouth and his lips were pulled back, revealing his white teeth. What was worse was that my oil smeared hands were losing their grip on the log which, inch by inch, was slipping through my fingers and with every inch; Fury's body sank lower and lower into the water. I felt myself cry out in frustration. There was nothing I could do to save him. My fingers finally gave way and the log rolled. Fury disappeared below the water and I knew it was the end; he was tied to the log and too exhausted to save himself anyway.

I cried out in anguish, and as my hands splashed around, frantically trying to get another grip on the log, I felt something beneath my feet. It was loose pebbles; we had finally reached the bank of the estuary. With a last surge of energy, I stood on legs like jelly and hauled the log over. Fury's body hung limp, its weight almost too much for me to keep up. Stella was still tied to the log and her eyes, as ever were watching me. The despair that filled me was almost too much to bear; but I wasn't ready to give up on Fury yet. I hauled on the log with all my might and pulled it into the shallow water where it beached and thankfully toppled slowly over, away from me, swinging Fury up and out of the river water. He lay, limp and motionless across the log, tied by the single piece of improvised rope I had made. It was Stella that was in trouble now though; the tilting of the log as it grounded had plunged her beneath the water.

I ran around and desperately tore at the knots securing the otter to the log. As the second one came away I lifted her in my arms and splashing water to left and right; ran ashore. I laid her more roughly than I had intended on the loose pebbles and turned my full attention back to Fury. If I undid the rope holding him, he would have just slid into the water so I had to work on him where he was. I stood with my legs straddled across the log and Fury both. I didn't really know what I was doing and it was hard to see clearly with the tears that I couldn't stop and the stinging of the oil. I felt for the point on top of his ribcage where I thought his heart might be. I had to try and get it going again. I had seen a programme about resuscitating a human and that involved pressing down rapidly on the ribs above the heart followed by mouth to mouth breathing; that was out as far as I could see but the first bit I was damn well going to try. I put one hand flat on his ribs and the other on top. I repeatedly pushed down sharply ten times then sat back to look... nothing. I tried again but twenty times in rapid succession - I had no idea if I was doing it hard or fast enough. After the second set, I noticed a trickle of water coming out of Fury's mouth, but still no sign of life. I tried again, thirty this time I decided and put more of my body weight into it. After about fifteen, water gushed out of the sides of Fury's mouth and he coughed, once, then again and again; his chest heaved under me and I collapsed, wrapping his great body in my arms. Fury was back.

I quickly got off of Fury, realising that what he could probably do without was my weight on top of him at this moment. His tongue hung out of the side of his mouth and he was so weak that he couldn't even raise his head. All that mattered to me though, was that the heart in that powerful chest was beating once more.

Chapter 23
Getting Back

It took me nearly an hour to untie Fury and drag him up the gentle beach we had landed on, just inside the mouth of the river's estuary. Eventually, the three of us lay next to each other; dirty, oil coated, soaking, cold and exhausted. The sun had been going down when we left the island, and now, it had almost dropped beneath the horizon and the gloom would soon become full night. There was nothing to do but lay there until a little strength returned.

Stella was so ill that she simply lay where she was, her bright eyes the only sign of life in the small body. It took Fury another twenty minutes before he tried and eventually managed to stagger to his feet. He came closer and licked my face before wandering around the beach, sniffing.

As I lay there, I was puzzled as to why no one had come to look for me. Molly would certainly have shouted out about my absence after I had been away for a couple of hours or so and with the volunteers and army there; why hadn't they come looking for me? I couldn't work it out; but the truth of it was that as they hadn't come yet, it was unlikely they would come anytime soon. We were on our own and I knew only too well how urgent was the need to get both Stella and Fury back to safety and medical treatment.

'First things first', I thought to myself; I was shaking and my teeth were chattering. Looking around, I realised we were no more than fifty metres from the point I had entered the river. Wearily, I dragged myself to my feet and shuffled along the bank until I reached my jacket, lying on a rock. I took off my soaking shirt and put on the jacket. Within a few minutes I felt life returning as my body started to heat up a bit. I wasn't warm but I was no longer freezing.

When I returned to Stella I panicked as her eyes were closed. For a moment I thought she had slipped away, but when I gently stroked the still oil-stained fur around her head; they opened again. They weren't as bright as before, I was sure. I knew in my heart that I didn't have much longer to get Stella the medical treatment she so desperately needed. Fury had returned and was sitting quietly next to Stella. His eyelids were drooping and his head was hanging low to the ground. We were a sorry state and the weariness from the last few days, the lack of sleep and the exertions of the last few hours was like a great weight on my back, about to crush me into the ground. Every movement was a struggle. I bent down and picked up Stella; she hung limply in my arms. 'Come on boy,' I said to Fury and without raising his head, he stood uncertainly and followed me on legs made of jelly.

By the time we had climbed the bluff and descended the other side I could barely keep standing, the slender body of the otter like a ten tonne weight in my arms. There was no way I could make it back to The Sanctuary without a few hours rest and Stella would not survive that long. What was I to do? It was only two miles but it might as well have been a hundred.

As I stood swaying, the last of the light fading fast, I suddenly thought about the highway. It ran parallel to the coast about half a mile inland I thought. Half a mile compared to two miles; it was a no-brainer. I turned inland and trudged like a zombie towards where I hoped the road would be. Through drooping eyelids I looked at a rock or tree ahead and counted the paces to get to it. Each object in front of me was a target to reach and I focused on just reaching the next one before choosing another. I don't know how long it took; I had to drape Stella over my shoulder before my arms gave out. Fury walked alongside me, continually bumping into my legs as he staggered along. We didn't make a sound. Before long it was completely dark. The sky was clear and speckled with a million stars, whilst a ghostly half moon gave just enough light to make out some things around me. I continually stumbled and had to stop every hundred yards or so to catch my breath.

That walk seemed to go on forever and I must have ended up walking whilst I was sleeping because the next thing I knew, a terrifying animal was howling at me and a dazzling white light burned my eyes. I turned, shielding my eyes with my free hand, expecting to feel the teeth of some terrible predator sink into my flesh. But the light was gone as suddenly as it had appeared and the roaring, howling noise receded into the distance.

I just stood there for a few moments trying to engage my brain and understand what was happening. As I looked down, I realised I was standing on a hard flat surface, unlike the dirt and rock I had been traipsing across for what seemed like hours. It was a road. My eyes widened as I realised I had stumbled straight onto the highway and the creature that had attacked me had been a car. It must have swerved to avoid me, blaring its horn as it passed. I had been very luck, I could have so easily been killed. I was shaking again, but this time it was the shock of my narrow escape that was causing it. Fury was lying at my feet. He didn't look like he was going to be going any further. I coaxed him to the side of the highway and lay Stella beside him for warmth; then I stood out in the middle of the highway and waited. It wasn't a busy road and it took a good ten minutes for another car to come into view in the distance. As it approached, I stood my ground and waved my arms frantically. I was wearing dark jeans and a dark coat, so the driver only saw me in the dark when his headlights illuminated me. The car screeched as the driver yanked the wheel hard and the car skidded sideways. I closed my eyes, sure it was going to hit me, but the squealing of the tyres stopped and as I cautiously opened my eyes, I saw the car, sideways on, stopped five metres in front of me.

Before I could move, the driver's door had opened and a figure was climbing out, 'What the hell do you think you're doing you young idiot?' it bellowed at me.

I slowly sank to my knees, unable to support my weight any longer. 'Please help us,' I whispered.

And then the man was by my side, picking me up and there was a woman's voice as well, 'Did he say, 'us'?' it asked. I raised my arm and pointed over to where Fury and Stella were lying. And that's the last I remember for a while.

I came round as my rescuers were helping me out of the car. I immediately recognised The Sanctuary. We were parked at the back, amongst the tents and other temporary buildings. It was brightly lit by portable lights and there were dozens of people going about their jobs, helping to save animals from the oil pollution. There were plenty of hands ready and willing to carry myself, Fury and Stella inside and I soon found myself in the kitchen with a mug of tea and a warm bath robe wrapped around me.

It was Molly I wanted to see. I wanted to let her know that Stella was alive, that I had brought her back. But she was not there. Gabe and Jen Munroe sat with me. 'Molly's gone,' Jen said. Her face was grim and she looked angry. 'Her step-father came and took her. She didn't want to go and we tried to convince him she was safe here but he insisted, then he got angry, said he was her legal guardian and dragged her off.' So that was why no one had come looking for me. Molly had not had time to tell anyone I had gone after Stella before that awful man had taken her away. And my parents had gone home, thinking I was fine at The Sanctuary and happy that I was sleeping there whilst this whole disaster unfolded.

Gabe and Jen were concerned about me, but I convinced them not to call my parents. I was fine... apart from the dirt and tiredness. I didn't tell them everything that had happened; I left out the island, just telling them I had found Stella on the bank of the river, and that Fury had gone into the water before I could stop him and got covered in oil too. They seemed to accept this and the next thing I wanted to know was; how were the patients?

'Fury is going to be fine,' said Gabe. 'His fur is going to take a lot of work to get clean, but he hasn't swallowed much oil and apart from some cream for his eyes, he just needs to rest. Stella is more serious I'm afraid. She has blood poisoning from all the oil inside her and her fur will take weeks to clean and get back its natural ability to keep her warm and buoyant when swimming.'

'Is she going to make it?' I asked. I couldn't keep the concern out of my voice.

'It's going to be touch and go,' said Jen. 'We'll do everything we can. The fact you got her here for treatment means she at least has a chance. If you hadn't found her, she'd be dead by now.'

There was nothing else for me to say or do, so I was packed off to bed for the rest of the night in the little room at the top of the house.

Part Four

Loose Ends

Chapter 24
Molly

It took another month for the worst of the oil to be cleared up. Some of it was surrounded by mile long booms and sucked up; some was dispersed by spraying it with special detergents. It took over a thousand people, working tirelessly on over fifty ships of varying sizes. The view from the lighthouse was like looking at the M25 on a busy day most of the time.

Clearing up the oil that had already reached the shore and saving as many of the hundreds of thousands of birds, mammals and fish that had been affected as possible took many months. There would be traces of oil on the southern coast of Nova Scotia for many years to come. I helped with that as much as I could at weekends and during school holidays, but the most important thing I had to do after getting back to Cranberry Cove with Stella was to fulfil my promise to Molly.

I wanted to go round and see her the very next day, after I had had a good night's sleep, a half hour shower to scrub off the oil and some nice, dry, warm clothes; but I didn't want to see her until I had certain news of Stella. I had to go to school as well. I had got away with a few days off to help with the initial disaster of the oil hitting the coast but now, mum and dad forced me to go back. I did, but there was no sign of Molly. It was good to see my friends but school just wasn't the same knowing how so many people were fighting to save the lives of the creatures that shared our coast back home. My mind wasn't on my work and I was counting the hours until I could climb on the bus and return to Peggy's Cove.

When I got back, Fury wasn't there to greet me; he was still at The Sanctuary. I scurried home to change and then ran all the way to Cranberry Cove. The shore was a hive of activity. There were gangs of people; oil company staff, government workmen and volunteers, wrapped in orange overalls, using great, wide spades to scoop the black, crude oil into barrels. I ran on, until I reached The Sanctuary. I immediately went to the shed where I knew Stella was being looked after. Inside, I went up to the pen she was in and my mouth dropped in stunned shock as I saw she wasn't there. Had the poor little thing finally succumbed to the poison during the night? I felt intense sadness for both Stella and maybe even more for my friend Molly who I knew would be heart-broken at the loss of her friend. 'Hi there Harry,' said a loud voice I recognised at once. I turned in time to see Ma coming into the shed, and there in her arms, wrapped in a thick towel was Stella. 'I've just been having another go at getting some of that darn'd stuff off of her. It's going to take quite a few more cleaning sessions yet but I reckon we're making headway.'

The relief I felt was unbelievable and I walked over to stroke Stella under her chin. She wrinkled her whiskers in response and looked at me with tiny eyes that seemed to have at least a little of their previous sparkle in them. 'Is she going to make it Ma?' I asked.

'You bet she is,' Ma boomed. 'Molly'll have her little playmate back, right as rain in a few weeks.'

'Thanks,' I said, with feeling. 'I'm going to tell Molly.'

The big, friendly woman looked like she was going to say something to me then, but instead she just nodded and gave me a thin smile.

My next stop was Fury, who was in a pen in another shed. Some of the oil had been cleaned from his fur, but he still looked sorry for himself and it was all he could do to crawl over to the wire mesh and feebly lick my fingers as I caressed his head. 'You'll be fine in a couple of days, boy,' I said softly. Fury whined quietly. It was obvious that the oil that had got into his system was making him feel really sick, but that would pass. He had been very lucky. With a last kiss on his wet nose, I left.

I ran all the way back to Peggy's Cove. Breathless and with an awful stitch running down my side, I stopped in front of Molly's house. Whilst I got my breath back, I looked at the place. It was uncared for and didn't look like it had been painted for years. It would take a good deal of money to fix it up I thought. Apprehensively, I climbed the rotting wooden steps up to the porch and rapped on the door. I waited but there was no answer. I didn't want to leave without letting Molly know Stella was safe, so, plucking up all my courage, I walked round to the back of the house. No houses in these parts had beautiful, manicured gardens like back in Britain, the weather, salty sea air and poorness of the soil meant that was almost impossible, But even by Nova Scotia standards, this yard was a mess; the few bushes were overgrown and the coarse grass was above waste high. It was topped off by piles of rubbish and a couple of old, part-dismantled car engines. Carefully stepping around the obstacles, I looked up. There were two windows in the upper floor, one was small and both were almost covered in dirt. The smallest was Molly's room I knew through our chats. I picked up a small stone and threw it. It took me a couple of goes before one rattled against the glass and moments later, I saw a faint movement in the darkness behind the grime.

The window swung outwards with a screech and Molly looked out. I immediately saw a livid purple bruise on her forehead and I felt the old anger surge up inside me. 'Are you alright?' I demanded in a voice more forceful than I had meant it to be. She just nodded.

'Can you come down?' I called. This time she shook her head.

'Did you find Stella?' Molly called in a voice so filled with desperation it made me want to cry.

'I did,' I called. 'She's at The Sanctuary. She's being looked after really well and she's going to be okay.'

Stella broke down and began to sob. She must have been beside herself with worry, both for Stella and for me and Fury. 'Thank you,' she managed to blurt out. 'Oh thank you. You can't know what that means to me.'

At that moment there was the sound of a car pulling up out front and Molly suddenly looked completely panicked. 'You've got to go,' she called. 'He'll go mad if he finds you here.'

'I don't care,' I called back. 'I'm not scared of that drunken, old bully.'

'But I am,' she replied in a small voice. I knew then how vulnerable my friend was in the clutches of that monster. She disappeared quickly from view and the window closed. I crept round the side of the house and waited for the front door to slam shut before making my escape. I prayed that I had given Molly the hope she needed to hold out for a while longer. A plan was forming in my mind.

It took three weeks before I could put my plan into action. The clean-up was in full swing and the end was in sight. There was time to look to the future; a future after filthy, poisonous crude oil and heaps of oil soaked, dead animals. Our imminent departure from the lighthouse to Halifax had been well and truly halted. After the Orion V disaster and the oil spill, the oil company had abandoned all its plans to force anyone to move out. Fury was back with me, as good as new and Stella had made a full recovery; she now ran around and swam in her little home, 'The Water Park,' with a new reinforced door to keep her in until the oil was completely gone. There had been no sign of Molly either at school, at The Sanctuary or around Peggy's Cove. Most worryingly of all, a 'For Sale' sign had gone up in the front yard of her house. But I had had to wait until the end of the disaster was within reach. Now was the time to make my move.

I went straight round to The Sou' Wester to see Sandy Banks. The restaurant was closed and had been since the oil had hit. There was no fresh fish at the moment and anyway, everyone was too busy helping in the clear up to want to go out to eat. I rang the bell and waited. Eventually Sandy opened the door, 'Well, if it ain't young Harry Medhurst. What can I do for you boy?' he asked, clearly happy to see me.

'Hello Sandy,' I said. 'I just had an idea I wanted to run past you. Can I come in?'

'Surely,' Sandy said and ushered me in. In no time at all I was seated in a booth with a mug of tea in my hands and old Sandy sitting opposite, eager to hear what I had to say. 'Well, what's on yer mind?' he asked, leaning back on the worn leather bench.

'It's been a hard time recently. This disaster has stretched everyone to the limit. The fishermen, anyone who volunteered to help - and that's just about everyone - and just about anyone with a business like you,' I said.

'Reckon I know that alright,' said Sandy bitterly. 'Can't open a seafood restaurant without no fish and they're not exactly queuing up to come in at the moment neither. Most people don't know if they've got a job, nor even a future here after this. Certainly not likely to spend their savings on eating out at any rate.'

'But we're getting through it aren't we?' I said. 'I mean, the worst of it has past, hopefully. There's still a mountain of work to do but the end's in sight. They're clearing the oil up; the number of oiled up animals has gone down drastically and the government is talking about compensation to help out everyone whose livelihoods have been affected.' I stopped for a moment to see what effect my words were having.

Sandy was looking reflective, massaging his chin with one hand. 'There's a lot in what you say; there does look to be light at the end of the tunnel. But what brings you to my door?'

'Well, when my family arrived in Peggy's Cove, I remember how you were so kind to us when we first came here. We really started to feel part of the community from that moment. And then on Christmas Day; It was all people from round here; a real get-together.' I could see that the germ of the idea was planting itself behind that coarse, suntanned face, just as I had hoped.

'A party like; a get together to show everyone there is a future after all this. Yes, that's what we need.' Sandy was looking quite excited at the idea he had come up with completely on his own. 'Here, in the ol' Sou' Wester; I could open it up and set up tables on the street; it's warm enough now. What about food though? I ain't got much fish, what with the oil.'

'That wouldn't be a problem.' I said quickly. 'If you provide the venue, just ask everyone to bring along a dish of something and a bottle to drink. It wouldn't cost you anything.' This really made Sandy's eyes light up.

'I'll do it!' he shouted, slapping his hands on the table. 'I'll put up some posters, ring around and put the word out. Next Saturday, that'll give everyone time to prepare.'

I left shortly after with Sandy Banks whistling loudly and shouting orders to his staff, already getting ready for the big event.

It was the end of June by this time and there was the hint of summer in the air. It was

Wednesday, and I had three days. There was much to do between going to school, helping at The Sanctuary and putting my plan into action. The most important thing was to have a conversation with Gabe and Jen Munroe. I did that on Thursday evening.

I had invited myself over for dinner with the two vets and as we sat around the kitchen table, I asked them a few probing questions, 'You haven't got children have you?' I asked innocently.

I knew they hadn't and I saw a look of sadness pass between them before Gabe said, 'No... No, we haven't Harry.'

'Didn't you want any?' I asked. I felt really rotten for pushing them about this but I had to.

'We would have loved to have children Harry,' said Jen, and I thought I could see tears forming in her eyes. 'But unfortunately we couldn't. It's just one of those things Harry. Sometimes couples want to have children but they can't. We've come to terms with it; that we've just got each other.' There was a profound grief in Jen's voice and I felt ashamed of myself for bringing the whole thing up, but it had to be done.

'I'm sorry,' I said, 'I didn't mean to upset you both.'

'That's alright Harry,' said Gabe with a wry smile. 'But why do you ask? I don't think you've ever shown any interest in our family life before.'

This was my cue. I had rehearsed the next words carefully, 'It's just that I think you'd make such wonderful parents. And this place; the animals, Cranberry Cove, it's like a wonderland for children. If you'd had any, they would have been so happy here.'

I had to stop there as Jen stood up and walked over to the sink, staring out of the window. I knew she was crying and I hated myself for making my friends feel like that.

'It's very kind of you to say so,' said Gabe, giving my hand a quick squeeze, 'But like I said, it's not going to happen, and anyway, we're too busy now. We're on call at any hour of the day or night. The time for a family has passed us by.'

I nodded slowly and finished eating dinner. We didn't mention it again and though we changed the subject, the mood was much more sombre than before.

The next thing I had to do was get a message to Molly. I wracked my brain for a way of talking to her, without confronting her step-father or making him suspicious. it came to me suddenly and I felt stupid at not having thought about it before; I could just phone her couldn't I? I knew they had a phone but I had never rung her in all the time I had known her. I found the local phone book at the lighthouse and soon discovered her number listed. The next step was to call, when I was sure her step-father was out.

It wasn't until Friday evening that I had a chance to go into Peggy's Cove. Just outside Ma's shop was a payphone that I would use. I walked along the street with Fury by my side and found a bench along the street from Molly's house. I had a good view of the front and could see their car on the drive. That evil man was at home. I settled down to wait.

It was an hour and a half later, when night had fallen that I saw the lights of their car start up and it reversed out and roared off, tyres screeching. I hurried back to the pay phone and dialled Molly's number. I had no idea if she had gone with him or not and when there was no answer after the twelfth ring I thought the worst. I hung up then tried again; still no answer. When I put the receiver down I thought carefully what to do. She probably wasn't there, but even if she was, would she answer the phone? I was sure her step-father wouldn't normally allow her to. But what if she thought it was an emergency? I picked up the receiver and rang again, someone trying to ring three times must want to get through urgently. I heard the phone ring at the other end; eight, ten, fifteen rings; I started to put the receiver down again when I heard a click and a frightened, tiny voice said, 'Hello,'

'Molly? It's me, Harry. How are you?' I spluttered anxiously.

'Harry?' the voice asked in surprise. 'Is it really you?'

'It is. Are you alright?' I asked again. Molly didn't answer that.

'I've missed you,' she whispered. 'How is Stella,' she added, the concern all too plain in her voice.

'She's fine,' I reassured her. 'But she really misses you.

'Does she? Does she really?' Molly whispered and the longing to believe me was clear.

'Yes,' I said. 'She's virtually ignoring the rest of us. Sort of gone on strike till you get back I think.' There was silence at the other end of the phone. 'What's going on Molly. You haven't been to school and I haven't seen you around at all.'

'He's keeping me here,' Molly said. Her voice was so frail sounding; it was only just recognisable as hers. 'He's put the house up for sale. When he gets an offer he'll take me away and all the money will go on drink. I don't know what he'll do to me then. I won't be any more use to him, he'll have taken everything my mum had and was meant to go to me. He won't let me out until the house is sold. I've not been outside since he took me from The Sanctuary, when you were looking for Stella. He hates me,' she was crying now. 'I'm so scared. What will happen to me? No one will know where I've gone and no one will care.'

I could feel the tears of anger and frustration in my own eyes. I sniffed them back, 'I care about you Molly and so do a lot of other people. I think I can help,' I said.

'How?' Molly asked. 'How can you help?'

'I've got a plan. I'm your friend Molly. I've been your friend since we first met. I saved Stella for you and I'm going to help you now. You believe that don't you?'

'Yes, yes, I believe you Harry,' she said and I was almost sure her voice was a little stronger.

'What does your step-father do on a Saturday?' I asked.

'Well... He goes out early afternoon to drink with his mates in Halifax, then comes back about seven in the evening and drinks himself stupid into the early hours.'

'Right, I'm coming round for you at six tomorrow night. Make sure you are dressed in your best clothes,' I stopped as I heard sniffling at the other end of the phone.

'I'm scared,' Molly said.

'I know you are,' I tried to reassure her. 'It'll be alright. You have to trust me. I have a plan and I'm going to get that man out of your life for good.'

'But what about the house? It's the last link I've got to my mother.'

'Just be ready at six tomorrow. Everything will be alright.' I couldn't tell her any more without risking the whole plan and I didn't want her to argue anymore, so I quickly put the phone down and walked home. I was full of apprehension. Would the plan I had thought out work? There was so much that could go wrong. I couldn't think like that. I had to stay strong and believe it would work out.

I spent a restless night and slept little. I awoke, tired with Fury licking my face. Mum was busy already, cooking a dish for the party at The Sou' Wester later. Everyone was talking about it. When I walked into Peggy's Cove, Sandy was busy decorating the restaurant with bunting. In Ma's store, the three people waiting to be served were all talking about what they were making and what they intended to wear. Even at The Sanctuary, Gabe and Jen were planning to go and there was the smell of something delicious cooking in the kitchen. Most of the tents erected during the clean-up after the oil spill had gone now and there were just a handful of volunteers left helping to look after the invalid animals still recovering and to deal with the odd bird or seal that was still brought in occasionally. All of them seemed dead set on attending the party. That was good.

I helped out at The Sanctuary for most of the day, with Fury at my side, mainly to pass the time and not think about what might happen later.

At five, I went home, showered and got changed. Before I left at quarter to six, I slipped an envelope into my pocket that had been hidden inside one of my school text books. I was meeting mum, dad and Sal at the party, so it was just me and Fury who made the walk back to Peggy's Cove and before I knew it, my watch said six and I was standing outside Molly's house. It was a pleasantly warm spring evening and there were already people walking down to The Sou' Wester.

There was no car in the drive so I walked up the dilapidated steps and rapped on the door. It opened after just a few seconds. Molly stood there. The bruise had gone from her forehead but she looked pale and painfully thin. Her clothes, though probably the best she owned were old and ragged. She wore jeans, a stained white blouse and a thin shawl that she hugged tightly around her shoulders; her arms were wrapped around her body as if trying to protect it. She gave me a shy smile, 'Hello Harry, I've missed you.'

I stepped forward and hugged her tightly, but after a moment she gasped and pushed me away. She looked to be in pain. I thought I knew why and my blood boiled. I could hear Fury growling from the roadside. It was as close as he would come to the house, tainted with the smell of that evil man.

'I won't be a minute,' I said and darted past Molly before she had time to protest. I quickly went into a dark room to one side and felt satisfied as I saw a grimy armchair in the centre of the room. It stank of stale cigarettes and the only other furniture in the room was a big TV and a table by the armchair holding several filthy glasses and a couple of half empty bottles. This was his lair; where he drank himself into a stupor before taking his anger out on poor Molly up in her tiny room.

Carefully, I took the letter out of my jacket pocket and carefully leant it against an empty glass on the table by the armchair. Whoever sat there would be sure to see it. On the envelope was written one word, 'Goodbye.'

I quickly made my way back to the door where I raised a hand to stop Molly asking what I had been up to. Quickly, I took her by the arm and led her down the steps. Fury wagged his tail and licked Molly's free hand before we started off for the party.

When we arrived at The Sou' Wester, the party was already in full swing. There must have been at least fifty people there; mostly from Peggy's Cove but also from the surrounding area and they were families with children and older relatives. There was laughter and talking and pop music playing in the background. The restaurant looked a treat and there were tables inside piled with food. Most people were in the street where long trestle tables had been set up with camp chairs. More people were arriving all the time. Mum, dad and Sal made their entry, making a fuss of Molly who they hadn't seen for weeks, as did everyone there. She was liked by all. I kept looking at my watch; it was quarter to seven by that time. I was feeling anxious. I hadn't seen the Munroes and they were vital to my plan. If they weren't here everything could go wildly wrong.

Before I knew it my watch said seven and I was sweating like mad. Molly kept close by me, her arms wrapped around herself constantly as if she was freezing.

Still no Munroes; my plan was unravelling and there was nothing I could do about it. My mouth had gone dry as the minutes ticked by.

I felt a tiny pull at my jacket and realised Molly had grasped me. I looked at her and saw her eyes wide with fear. I turned to look where she was looking and there, careering down the street was her step-father's car. It swerved crazily as it came and I knew he must be drunk as a skunk, but that would just make him more dangerous.

The panic was rising inside me. Where were the Munroes? I didn't move from where we were standing near the edge of the crowd of partygoers. It had been vital that he should see Molly as he passed. The car was clearly heading for the highway, but suddenly, just as it passed the restaurant it skidded to a halt, ending up sideways in the road. The door opened and Mason Brook stumbled out. There was a baseball bat in one of his hands.

The crowd of partygoers had fallen silent and everybody was watching. 'Where is she?' Brook slurred. Nobody moved or said anything. 'Come over here girl or it'll be worse for you.' Brook staggered forward as he caught sight of Molly who was standing behind me. This was it. 'Thought you could just up and leave did you? Well you're coming back with me. Come on.'

I felt Molly start to move from behind me and she began to shuffle towards her step-father. 'Don't go,' I begged her in a whisper.

Molly turned her head and looked at me, 'Where else have I got to go?'

Brook was impatient; he reached out and grabbed molly by her arm, pulling her forward; she stumbled and fell. As she did, the shawl she had been holding around herself so tightly slipped and fell. There was a collective gasp from the crowd of local people; for as the shawl dropped, it revealed the back of Molly's dress, which was cut quite low at the back, and there, visible for all to see was a livid red and purple bruise. It was straight and ran from her shoulder down, at an angle towards her other shoulder. The mark looked angry and recent. It could only have been caused by a stick or a belt. 'Stop right there Brook!' a powerful voice from the back of the crowd boomed.

I recognised the voice and the crowd moved aside as the great bulk of Gabe Munroe pushed itself to the front. Behind him was Jen and her eyes were burning. Brook was standing stock still, looking from Molly on the ground in front of him to the Munroes behind. He didn't say anything. 'What have you done to that poor girl?' Jen cried in a voice full of accusation.

'It ain't none of your business,' Brook said sullenly. No one else had moved but there was a very different feeling to the gathering now.

The high spirits had turned to anger and what Mason Brook did next signalled the end of him. He reached down and yanked on Molly's arm, but she resisted and shouted at his face, 'I'm not going anywhere with you! I hate you!'

Brook's face turned red and he raised his hand to hit her. Before his hand had barely begun to swing down, a blur flew across the street and Fury hit Brook sending him flying. Fury grasped Brook's arm and shook for all he was worth. As this was going on, Jen Munroe rushed forward and scooped Molly up into her arms, whilst Gabe strode up and stood over Brook who was screaming for someone to get Fury off of him. I whistled and called his name sharply. Instantly, Fury let him go and trotted over to my side.

Brook tried to get to his feet, but Gabe pushed him back down with one of his bear like fists. 'You just stay there,' he said in a cold, hard voice. 'Someone call the police,' he added over his shoulder.

That was the last I saw of Molly for a few days. Jen Munroe took her into the restaurant to check her over and they called an ambulance after that. I saw Jen briefly and her face was drained of all colour.

The Royal Canadian Mounted Police took Mason Brook away and the whole crowd cheered as he was handcuffed and driven off.

Once everyone knew that Molly was safely on her way to hospital and Brook off to jail, the party started up again. It wasn't quite as jolly as before and most people were talking about Molly and cursing themselves for not having done anything about the brute before, but it was still a celebration of a new beginning; for the village after the oil spill and just maybe for Molly as well.

My plan was nowhere near finished. I hoped that Molly would never have to return to her step-father, but exactly what would happen to her was still very uncertain. I went into the restaurant after Molly had gone to hospital and managed to find a seat just behind Gabe and Jen Munroe. I listened carefully, and this is what I heard:

Jen: That poor girl.

Gabe: I know. I can't believe what she must have been through. Why didn't we do something about it?

Jen: We knew he was a bit of a swine and she was unhappy, but we had no idea he was mistreating her like this.

241

Gabe: What's going to happen to her now? With him gone, she has no one around here. It could be an orphanage.

Jen: Oh, no... no Gabe. We can't let that happen. Can't we help? Couldn't we look after her?

Gabe: Well... I suppose we could. We could find out if they'd let us at least. Are you sure Jen?

I stood up and went to find mum, dad and Sal just there, with a secret smile on my face. Just maybe my plan would work after all.

It was six weeks later before Molly returned to us at Peggy's Cove. She looked much better; her skin looked a healthy colour and she walked like she wasn't scared any more. Even her clothes were more colourful and newer.

I sat with her on the first evening of her return, on the headland above Cranberry Cove; away from the beach which still showed the signs of pollution. The sun shone down warmly and in front of us Fury was capering around, barking and snapping in a playful way at Stella, who darted back and forth between his legs.

We didn't speak much, but I knew that Molly was happy at last. She had moved her few belongings into The Sanctuary where she was to become part of the Munroe family. Gabe and Jen were going through the drawn out process of adopting Molly and the court, which had already put her step-father in jail for

242

a good long time, had assured her that her mother's house would be safe and given to her when she was old enough.

It truly had been an adventure coming to Canada, and although I still thought of my old life back in Britain often, it was Peggy's Cove where my heart now lay. If so much could happen in just a few short months here, I could hardly imagine what might await me in the years to come. I looked forward to finding out though.

Printed in Great Britain
by Amazon